THE WORLD OF
NORM
MAY REQUIRE BATTERIES

ORCHARD BOOKS
338 Euston Road, London NW1 3BH
Orchard Books Australia
Level 17/207 Kent Street, Sydney, NSW 2000

First published in 2013 by Orchard Books

A Paperback Original

ISBN 978 1 40832 614 5

A CIP catalogue record for this book is available from the British Library.

1 3 5 7 9 10 8 6 4 2

Printed in Great Britain

Orchard Books is a division of Hachette Children's Books,
an Hachette UK company.

www.hachette.co.uk

JONATHAN MERES

THE WORLD OF
NORM
MAY REQUIRE BATTERIES

ORCHARD

To Norms everywhere.

CHAPTER 1

Norm knew it was going to be one of those days when he got out of bed and trod on something he shouldn't have.

"Ow!" said a muffled voice. "Get off me!"

Norm looked down to see Brian lying on the floor, with the rug pulled up over his chin.

"What are you doing in my bedroom, Norman?" said Brian.

"Uh?" said Norm. "What do you mean, what am I doing in **your** bedroom? What are you doing in **mine**, you little freak?"

"What?" said Brian, propping himself up on one elbow and looking around. "Oh, right. Yeah. I must have got lost."

Norm regarded his middle brother with a mixture of curiosity and irritation. But mainly irritation. "What do you mean, lost?"

Brian thought for a moment. "Well, I must have got up to go to the toilet – then couldn't find my way back, or something."

Norm sighed. How could you get lost in a house the size of a flipping shoebox? OK, so it was only a few months since they'd moved here. But even so, what kind of doughnut couldn't even find their way back to their own flipping bedroom, wondered Norm (conveniently forgetting that it wasn't all that long since he himself had narrowly avoided peeing in his dad's wardrobe).

Actually, it was quite funny thinking about it, thought Norm, thinking about it. He'd heard of people getting out on the **wrong** side of bed before. He'd definitely got out on the **right** side. He'd just trodden on his brother!

"What?" said Brian, standing up and stretching.

"What do you mean, what?" said Norm.

"I asked first," said Brian, straightening the rug.

Norm was getting confused. "Asked what first?"

"What?" said Brian.

"What?" said Norm.

"I asked **what**, first," said Brian. "Then you asked what did I mean, what?"

Norm had only just woken up, but already he was beginning to wish he hadn't bothered. What on earth was Brian going on about? More importantly, **why** was he going on about it? It really was **much** too early for this.

"Oh, just clear off, Brian," said Norm, getting back into bed and wrapping the duvet tightly around himself until only his face was visible.

Brian couldn't help giggling.

"What's so funny?" snapped Norm.

"You look like a caterpillar," said Brian.

"Oh yeah?" said Norm. "Well, you look like a...a...a..."

"A what?" said Brian expectantly.

Norm couldn't think what Brian looked like. But whatever it was, it was extremely annoying. "Just go away, will you? Leave me in peace."

"But..." began Brian.

"But seriously," said Norm, cutting him off. "Go away, Brian. You've got ten seconds."

"But..." tried Brian again.

"My mistake," said Norm. "You've got **three seconds.**
>   **Two...**
>   **One...**"

"Time to get up, boys!" called Norm's dad from the bottom of the stairs.

"Uh?" said Norm. "Why didn't you tell me, Brian?"

"I was trying to," said Brian.

"What?"

"That's what I was **trying** to tell you."

"Oh, right," said Norm.

"You're welcome," said Brian, heading for the door.

"You up yet?" called Norm's dad.

"I am, Dad!" called Brian. "But Norman isn't!"

Norm glared venomously after Brian. But it was a waste of a perfectly good glare. Brian had already disappeared.

A hush descended on the room once more. A sliver of daylight pierced a crack in the curtains, illuminating a poster on the wall of a mountain biker frozen in midair. From the kitchen came the sound of early-morning radio – music, jingles and endless traffic reports about places Norm had never even heard of, let alone been to.

"Ah, **there** you are!" said Norm's dad from the doorway.

"Just a minute, Dad," grunted Norm.

"Not you, Norman," said Norm's dad. "I'm talking to Dave!"

Norm rolled over to see his little brother lying on the bed, next to him.

"Gordon Bennet!" said Norm. "Doesn't anyone sleep in their own flipping bed round here?"

"Language," yawned Dave, waking up.

"How long have you been there?" said Norm.

"No idea," said Dave.

"I think someone's been sleepwalking," chuckled Norm's dad.

"Don't remember," said Dave.

"Well, you wouldn't, would you?" said Norm. "That's why it's called sleepwalking, you doughnut. If you remembered, that would just be walking."

"You look like a caterpillar," said Dave.

"Yeah, whatever," said Norm.

"In your own time then," said Norm's dad, leaning on the doorframe, arms folded.

"What?" said Norm.

"Get up!" said Norm's dad.

"'Kay, Dad," said Dave, getting up and leaving the room.

"Good boy," said Norm's dad.

From behind his dad's back, Dave stuck his tongue out at Norm. In full view of his dad, Norm stuck his tongue out at Dave.

"Stop that, Norman," said Norm's dad.

"But Dave did it to me!" said Norm.

"I don't care!" said Norm's dad. "You're twelve years old!"

"Nearly thirteen," muttered Norm.

"Exactly!" said Norm's dad. "Old enough to know better! Now are you going to get up, or what?"

Norm thought for a moment. Was he going to get up, or what? "What if I don't?"

"Simple," said Norm's dad with a shrug of his shoulders. "You'll be late for school. And you wouldn't want that, would you?"

"You'd think," muttered Norm.

"What was that, Norman?"

"Er, I said I think you're absolutely right, Dad," said Norm. "I wouldn't want that."

"Excellent," said Norm's dad. "Do I need to wait here?"

"No, I'm getting up, Dad," said Norm.

"Promise?"

"Promise, Dad."

"OK, see you in a minute then," said Norm's dad, heading back downstairs.

Norm briefly thought about going back to sleep for a few more minutes. The trouble was that his stomach – traditionally an even slower starter than the rest of him – had finally woken up as well. And once Norm's stomach had woken up, there was no point staying in bed a second longer.

Norm sat up and got out of bed on the **other** side. This time, however, it was most definitely the **wrong** side of bed. For the second time that day, Norm trod on something he shouldn't have. Only this time, he **really** shouldn't have trodden on it. Certainly not without socks or slippers on anyway. He didn't need to look to know what it was either. But he still did.

"Phwoar! That is dis-flipping-gusting!" said Norm, wafting his hand in front of his face. "Stupid dog!"

"Woof!" went John from somewhere beneath the bed.

"Gordon flipping Bennet!" said Norm. "Don't tell me **you've** been sleeping here as well!"

"Woof!" went John again.

"What's **your** excuse?" said Norm. "No, don't tell me. You had a nightmare, right?"

"Norman?" called Norm's dad from the foot of the stairs.

"Coming, Dad!" called Norm, hopping towards the door.

CHAPTER 2

It was still a good five minutes before Norm finally appeared in the kitchen.

"What kept you?" said Norm's dad, the vein on the side of his head beginning to throb – a sure-fire sign that he was starting to get a bit stressed. Not that Norm ever noticed.

"Do you really want to know?" said Norm, sitting down at the table and helping himself to a bowl of supermarket own-brand Coco Pops.

"Er, yes, I do, actually," said Norm's dad between mouthfuls of toast and marmalade.

"I trod in some poo," said Norm.

Norm's dad pulled a face. "What?"

"I trod in some poo and had to wash it off in the bath," said Norm casually.

"Do you mind?" said Norm's dad. "Some of us are trying to eat here!"

"But you said you wanted to..."

"I don't care **what** I said, Norman. I've changed my mind."

"But..."

"No buts," said Norm's dad.

Brian giggled.

"Shut up, Brian, you freak!" hissed Norm. "It's all your fault anyway!"

Brian pulled a face. "What?"

"It's *your* stupid dog!" said Norm.

"Oh, right, it's **dog** poo!" said Brian. "I thought you meant it was..."

"Sssssh!" said Norm's dad. "That's enough!"

"And John's not stupid, either, by the way," said Brian.

"Yeah, he is," said Norm. "He can't even understand English."

"That's because he's Polish!" said Brian indignantly.

"I said that's enough!" said Norm's dad.

"Yeah, Brian," sneered Dave.

"Shut up, Dave," said Brian.

"Shut up, Brian," said Norm.

"Yeah, Brian," sneered Dave.

"I'm warning you!" said Norm's dad. "**All** of you. Just get on with your breakfast quietly or you'll be late for school."

"And we wouldn't want that," muttered Norm.

"What was that, Norman?"

"Nothing, Dad," said Norm.

"Good," said Norm's dad. "Because one more peep out of any of you and there'll be no pocket money this week."

That did the trick. There were no more peeps. Frankly, thought Norm, there would've been no peeps in the first place had he known that this week's pocket money was at stake. They'd only recently started getting it again. It wasn't very much. But every little helped and all that. Norm certainly had no intention of blowing it now.

The time – according to the DJ on the radio – was just coming up to ten past eight. Norm liked to be out the door by twenty past at the latest. Well, strictly speaking, his mum and dad liked him to be out the door by twenty past at the latest. If it was up to Norm he wouldn't ever leave the house until thirty seconds before school was due to start. Possibly even later if he'd got maths first period.

Norm munched on a mouthful of own-brand Coco Pops. There was something not quite right. Something not quite the same as usual. But what? He just couldn't seem to put his finger on it.

"Yes, Brian? What is it?" said Norm's dad.

Norm swivelled round to see his middle brother with his hand in the air, as if he was in class already. Seemingly he had no intention of jeopardising his pocket money, either.

"Where's Mum?"

So *that* was it, thought Norm. His mum wasn't there. He knew there was **something** different!

"She's at work," said Norm's dad.

Work? thought Norm. Since when did his mum work? She might have flipping said!

"She got a call late last night."

"Who from?" said Brian.

"A friend of hers who runs a café in town," said Norm's dad.

Norm was gobsmacked. His mum had a friend? No one told him anything!

"Not Strictly Come Munching?" said Dave, without bothering to put his hand up first.

Norm's dad nodded.

"Awesome!" said Dave. "Does that mean we get free cakes?"

"We'll see how it goes," laughed Norm's dad. "She's just helping out while someone's off sick."

"Talking about going," said Brian, getting up from the table and heading for the door.

"Good boy, Brian," said Norm's dad.

"Creep," muttered Norm under his breath, as first Brian and then Dave disappeared up the stairs to brush their teeth and get ready for school.

"So?" said Norm's dad once they were gone.

"So, what?" said Norm.

"What do you think?"

"About what, Dad?"

"Your mum, working?"

"Oh, I see," said Norm. "No, that's great, Dad. Really great."

Sniff
Sniff

"You're right actually, Norman. It **is** great. She has to be able to afford all that stuff she buys off the telly somehow!"

Norm's dad suddenly wrinkled his nose, picked up the milk

jug and sniffed a couple of times. "Is it me, or is this off?"

That's not the milk you can smell, thought Norm, making a mental note to give his foot another wash before he left for school.

CHAPTER 3

One of the good things about moving house as far as Norm was concerned – actually, the **only** good thing about moving house as far as Norm was concerned – was that he didn't have to move school as well. On top of everything else – postage stamp-sized room, paper-thin walls, only one toilet etc. etc. – that really would have been **too** much to bear. Not that Norm particularly liked his school. Far from it in fact. But at least it meant he still went to the same school as his best friend, Mikey.

"You're late," said Mikey, already waiting at the end of his drive as Norm pedalled round the corner on his bike.

"You always say that," said Norm, slowing down and stopping.

"That's because you're always late," said Mikey.

It was a fair point, thought Norm. He **was** always late. "It's not my fault."

Mikey pulled a face. "Whose fault is it, then?"

"Isn't it obvious?" said Norm.

"No," said Mikey.

"It's my mum and dad's fault!" said Norm. "For moving further away!"

"Oh right, I see," said Mikey. "And you wouldn't think of maybe allowing a bit more time?"

Norm laughed. "Good one, Mikey."

"What?" said Mikey, straight-faced.

"You're not actually serious, are you?" said Norm. "You honestly expect me to get up earlier just because it takes longer to get to school?"

"Erm, well…"

"You do, don't you?" said Norm. "Whose flipping side are you on, Mikey?"

Mikey knew better than to try and argue with Norm when he was in a mood like this. And a mood like this was pretty much Norm's default setting these days. Besides, if they didn't get a shift on, they were going to be even later.

"Come on," said Mikey, setting off down the street.

Norm shook his head and followed after him.

"UNBELIEVABLE. UNBE-FLIPPING-LIEVABLE."

They cycled on in silence for a few minutes – Mikey keen to get to school on time, Norm still slightly miffed that Mikey had had the audacity to suggest that he actually spent even less time in bed. But silences between Norm and Mikey rarely lasted. And this one was no different.

"What have we got first period?" said Norm.

"You mean you don't know?" said Mikey.

"I'm just testing you," said Norm.

"What?" said Mikey.

"Course I don't flipping know, Mikey! Why do you think I'm flipping asking?"

"Oh, right," said Mikey. "Geography."

Norm sighed. "Can't see the point."

"Of what?"

"Geography."

Mikey glanced across at Norm, pedalling alongside him. "You can't see the point of geography?"

"It's well boring."

"No, it's not, Norm. I've got this brilliant app for my iPad that..."

Norm immediately jammed on his brakes and skidded to a halt. Mikey slowed down more sedately before turning round and heading back along the street, towards Norm.

"What is it?" said Mikey, suddenly concerned.

"iPad?" said Norm.

"Ah," said Mikey. "Erm..."

"You've got an iPad? An actual iPad?"

"I was going to tell you, Norm," said Mikey sheepishly. "Honest."

"Really?" said Norm.

Mikey nodded.

"Yeah, well, there's no need now, is there, Mikey?"

Norm knew there was no need for Mikey to tell him in the *first* place. There was no actual legal obligation to tell him at all. Why *should* Mikey tell him he'd got an iPad just because they were best friends? He didn't have to if he didn't want to. Norm knew that. Mikey knew that. Norm knew that Mikey knew that. Mikey knew that Norm knew that he knew that. But Mikey was very sensitive to the fact that Norm's family had been a bit strapped for cash lately and that Norm's dad was currently out of a job. Which was why he hadn't told Norm earlier. But he was always going to at some point. When the time was right. Whenever that was.

"I've not just been *given* it, Norm," said Mikey. "It wasn't a present!"

Norm shrugged. "Whatever."

"I had to put some of my own money towards it!"

But Norm wasn't listening any more. The words were going straight in one ear and right back out the other. Frankly, Mikey could have been talking Bulgarian for all Norm knew. Or cared for that matter. All Norm could think about was the fact that Mikey had an iPad – and he didn't. And that wasn't just unfair – that was very unfair indeed.

"We'd better get going," said Mikey, setting off again.

Norm didn't say anything – but followed all the same.

The silence lasted a bit longer this time. But this time it was Mikey who eventually broke it.

"What did you get for your maths homework, Norm?"

"What?" said Norm.

"What did you get for your maths homework?" repeated Mikey.

Norm thought for a moment. "Nothing."

"Nothing?" said Mikey. "As in 'zero'?"

"As in 'I haven't done it'," said Norm.

"Oh, right," said Mikey. "Why not?"

"Couldn't be bothered."

"You couldn't be bothered?"

"I Forgot, Mikey, OK?"

snapped Norm.

"OK, OK," said Mikey. "Sorry I asked!"

"So am I," muttered Norm.

"What are you going to do?" said Mikey.

"Dunno," said Norm. "There's not a lot I *can* do, is there? We're here now!"

The words were scarcely out of Norm's mouth before he and Mikey turned into the school entrance and the bell rang for registration.

"Bet she'll go mad," said Mikey.

"Who? Marge?" said Norm.

Mikey nodded.

"She's not got much further to go," said Norm. "She's halfway there already."

Mikey couldn't help laughing. "Well, I wouldn't like to be in your shoes, Norm."

"You really wouldn't, Mikey," said Norm, recalling what he'd accidentally trodden in less than an hour before. "Trust me."

CHAPTER 4

As things turned out, Marge – or to give her her proper title, Mrs Simpson – didn't actually go mad at all. In fact, as things turned out, she was remarkably calm.

"So, Norman."

"Yeah?"

"Excuse me?" said Mrs Simpson, raising an eyebrow.

"I mean, yeah, Marge?" said Norm. "I mean, yes, Marge? I mean, yes, Mrs Simpson?"

There were some scattered outbreaks of giggling round the

class that Mrs Simpson chose to ignore. She was well aware what her nickname was. At least it showed a **bit** of imagination. It was certainly a lot more original than simply adding a 'y' onto the end of your surname, which seemed to be the fate of most teachers. She'd even entered into the spirit once by coming to school on dress-down day with yellow face paint and a tall blue wig.

"What are we going to do with you?"

Norm thought for a moment. What were they going to do with him? He had no idea what they were going to do with him. And who were **they** anyway?

"It's a rhetorical question, Norman," said Mrs Simpson.

Norm pulled a face.

"It means I'm not really expecting an answer."

Uh? thought Norm. If she wasn't expecting an answer, why flipping ask?

"It's not the first time, is it?" said Mrs Simpson.

Norm was confused. "What? That you haven't expected an answer?"

There was another outbreak of giggling that again Mrs Simpson chose to ignore.

"I mean, it's not the first time you haven't done your homework."

"Oh, right," said Norm. "Erm, no, it's not. No."

"In fact," said Mrs Simpson, "I'd say it was probably about the fifth time."

Fifth time? thought Norm. It was more than that. For a maths teacher, Mrs Simpson wasn't much cop at counting. But Norm decided not to say anything.

"What's wrong, Norman?"

Norm wasn't sure whether to answer or not. "Er, is that a historical question, Mrs Simpson?"

Mrs Simpson almost smiled. "Rhetorical."

"Yeah, one of those," said Norm.

"No, Norman, it's not a rhetorical question," said Mrs Simpson. "Is something wrong?"

Was something wrong? thought Norm. Flipping right there was something wrong! He'd got out of bed and trodden in some dog poo. His brothers seemed determined to move into his room with him. And to top it all, he'd just discovered that Mikey had gone and got a flipping iPad! How much more wrong could things actually be?

"What I mean is, is there a **reason** you're not doing your homework?" said Mrs Simpson.

"A reason?" said Norm.

Mrs Simpson nodded.

"I just keep forgetting."

"Forgetting?"

"Yeah," said Norm. "I mean, yes, Mrs Simpson."

"I'm afraid that's not a good enough excuse, Norman," said Mrs Simpson. "You'll have to do better than that. A lot better."

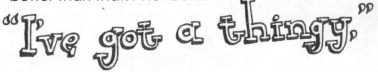

said Norm, prompting more giggling.

"A thingy?"

"Yeah," said Norm. "A whatsit."

"A whatsit?" said Mrs Simpson.

"Yeah, you know," said Norm.

"I'm afraid I don't know, Norman."

"A syndrome!" said Norm, finally finding the word he'd been looking for. "I've got a syndrome!"

"Oh, have you now?" said Mrs Simpson. "And what syndrome's that, then?"

Norm hesitated whilst he quickly thought of one. "ASDH."

"ASDH?" said Mrs Simpson. "And what does that stand for?"

"A Severe Dislike of Homework," said Norm.

That did it. The whole class – including Mrs Simpson – suddenly burst out laughing.

titter titter tee hee!

"Very good, Norman," said Mrs Simpson. "If I were your English teacher and this were a creative writing exercise I'd give you top marks. But unfortunately for you, I'm not and it's not. But what I **can** give you is a letter for your parents."

"A letter?" said Norm. "What kind of letter?"

"A letter of concern," said Mrs Simpson, opening a drawer in a filing cabinet and rummaging about before producing a sheet of paper. "It's standard procedure, Norman. You give me no alternative, I'm afraid."

Brilliant, thought Norm. Just what he flipping needed. His mum and dad were going to love this!

"Unless..." began Norm.

"Sorry?" said Mrs Simpson, writing on the sheet of paper, folding it and popping it in an envelope.

"Unless you choose to punish me in some other way, Mrs Simpson?"

"Such as?" said Mrs Simpson.

"Ooh, I dunno," said Norm. "Lines? Detention? I really don't mind. It's up to you."

"Well, that's very kind of you, Norman, but a letter usually does the trick. Normally nips it in the bud."

Uh? thought Norm. Nip what in the bud? What was this? Maths or flipping biology?

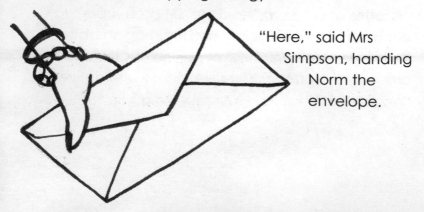

"Here," said Mrs Simpson, handing Norm the envelope.

"Thanks," said Norm.

"Don't 'forget' to give it to them," said Mrs Simpson, making speech marks in the air with her fingers.

"Course not," said Norm.

"You'd be surprised at the number of these letters that never actually make it home."

I bet I flipping wouldn't, thought Norm.

"There's an app..." blurted Mikey, before suddenly stopping himself.

"What was that, Michael?" said Mrs Simpson.

"Er, nothing," said Mikey, glancing nervously across at Norm.

"No, I insist," said Mrs Simpson. "Do go on, Michael."

"Yes, *Michael*," muttered Norm. "Do go on."

"Erm, well, I was just going to say that there's this app you can get for your iPad that reminds you to do your homework," mumbled Mikey.

"Very good," said Mrs Simpson.

"As long as you remember to download it," said Norm. "Mind you, there's probably an app to remind you to do that as well, isn't there, *Michael?*"

"Do I detect a note of jealousy, Norman?" said Mrs Simpson.

"No, no," said Norm with a dismissive shrug of his shoulders.

But Mrs Simpson was right and Norm knew it. Except it wasn't just a *note* of jealousy. It was a whole flipping symphony.

CHAPTER 5

The silence between Norm and Mikey on the way back from school was almost deafening. And this time it looked like it was going to last. Mikey glanced across at Norm a couple of times as they cycled along, but it soon became clear that Norm was in no mood for small talk. Or big talk. Or any kind of talk in between for that matter.

"See you then, Norm," said Mikey when they reached the end of Mikey's road and he turned towards his house.

"Wouldn't count on it," muttered Norm darkly, carrying on down the street by himself.

Norm was faced with a choice. He could either go straight home the quickest and most direct way, or he could take the slightly longer route, via the allotments. One of the advantages of going via the allotments was that Norm got to ride the trail through the woods. The other advantage was that there was a very good chance he'd get to see Grandpa.

It wasn't exactly a tough choice to make. The mood Norm was in, getting home as quickly as possible was never really an option. And besides, he fancied the idea of burning some rubber on his bike. Or if not actually **burning** some rubber, at least singeing it slightly.

There was nothing Norm liked better than to get on his bike and ride. Whether it was jumping off the steps in the shopping precinct,

bombing down a hill

or just practising wheelies on the drive, Norm lived and breathed biking. When he wasn't biking, he was *thinking* about biking. When he wasn't *thinking* about biking, he was *dreaming* about biking. It was the one thing Norm was truly passionate about. The one thing he was only too happy to fully focus on. The one thing that demanded his total concentration. Biking for Norm wasn't just exciting and fun. It meant he could switch off the part of his brain that was normally chock-a-block full of clutter and rubbish stuff.

Not today though. Today Norm couldn't concentrate for toffee. Not on biking he couldn't anyway. The only thing Norm could concentrate on today was the fact that Mikey had an iPad – and *he* flipping didn't! It wasn't flipping fair, thought Norm, misjudging a corner and nearly crashing into a tree. It just wasn't flipping fair at all.

With a sigh of frustration, Norm got off his bike and began pushing instead. It felt like he'd never *been* on a bike before. Frankly, thought Norm, the way he was feeling, if someone had offered to swap him an iPad for his bike there and then, he'd have flipping taken it. He probably didn't even need a bike any more anyway. There was probably some flipping app you could get instead.

"Well, well, well," said Grandpa, emerging from his shed in the allotments when Norm appeared a few minutes later. "Fancy seeing you here."

"Fancy seeing you here, Grandpa," said Norm gloomily.

Grandpa studied Norm for a moment. "Cheer up, Norman. It might never happen."

"Just flipping did," said Norm.

"What do you mean?" said Grandpa.

"It already **has** happened," said Norm.

"Oh right, I see," said Grandpa. "Like that, is it?"

Norm nodded but said nothing.

"Are you going to tell me about it, or just stand there like a complete lemon?" said Grandpa.

"You won't understand, Grandpa," said Norm. "No offence."

"None taken," said Grandpa, his eyes crinkling ever so slightly in the corners – the closest Grandpa ever got to smiling.

"Mikey's got something."

"Oh dear," said Grandpa. "I hope it's not catching."

"What?" said Norm. "No, I don't mean that, Grandpa. I mean he's got something I wish *I'd* got."

"Oh, I see," said Grandpa.

"Jammy doughnut."

Grandpa pulled a face. "Mikey's got a jammy doughnut?"

"He hasn't **got** one!" said Norm. "He **is** one!"

"Oh, right," said Grandpa. "I was going to say if that's all it was, I'd give you some money to buy one."

Norm did his best to raise a smile. "Thanks, Grandpa."

"Don't mention it," said Grandpa. "So the green-eyed monster's raising its ugly head again, is it?"

It was fair to say Norm no longer had any idea what Grandpa was on about. Not that he'd had much idea in the first place. "Sorry, Grandpa, what?"

"You're jealous."

"Oh, right," said Norm. "Yeah. Very."

"Fair enough," said Grandpa.

"Really?" said Norm. "But I thought…"

"What?" said Grandpa.

"Isn't jealousy, like, one of the Seven Deadly Dwarves or something?"

"You mean sins?" said Grandpa, his eyes crinkling slightly in the corners again.

"Whatever," said Norm.

"Perfectly natural if you ask me," said Grandpa.

"To be jealous?" said Norm.

"Of course," said Grandpa. "Completely normal."

This, thought Norm, was why he liked talking to Grandpa so much. Well – **one** of the reasons he liked talking to Grandpa so much, anyway. It never ever felt like Grandpa was preaching, or lecturing, or somehow trying to brainwash him into his way of thinking like most grown-ups did.

"So why won't I understand?" said Grandpa. "What's Mikey got that you wish **you'd** got?"

"It's called an iPad," said Norm.

Grandpa hesitated ever so slightly. Not that Norm noticed. "An iPad, eh? Hmm."

Norm nodded.

"What version?"

What? thought Norm. What **version**? He hadn't expected Grandpa to know what an iPad **was** – let alone that you could get different versions!

"But..." began Norm.

"But what?" said Grandpa.

"I didn't think you'd..."

"What?" said Grandpa.

"Nothing, Grandpa."

"I'm not as daft as I look, am I, Norman?"

Norm laughed nervously. "No, Grandpa."

Grandpa fixed Norm with a stare. "What? So you think I look daft, then, do you?"

"No, no! That's not what I meant, Grandpa!"

Grandpa's eyes crinkled in the corners again. "You want my advice?"

Norm shrugged. "If you want."

"Don't listen to advice," said Grandpa.

"What?" said Norm.

"Don't listen to advice," said Grandpa. "That's my advice."

Norm tried to make sense of what Grandpa had just said. But obviously not hard enough.

"What I'm saying, Norman, is – sure, listen to what other people have got to say. But at the end of the day, you have to make your own mind up."

Norm was still none the wiser. "What's this got to do with iPads, Grandpa?"

Grandpa thought for a moment. "Absolutely nothing."

But before the conversation could get any weirder, Norm's phone rang.

"Hi, Mum," he said, fishing it out of his pocket and answering. "'Kay, Mum. Bye, Mum."

"Who was that?" said Grandpa as Norm pocketed his phone again and got on his bike.

"Mum," blurted Norm before he could stop himself.

Grandpa's eyes crinkled in the corners.

"Very funny, Grandpa," said Norm, disappearing down the path towards the gate. "Gotta go. She's forgotten something."

"Get one with more memory!" called Grandpa. "An iPad, I mean! Not a mum!"

But it was too late. Norm had already gone.

CHAPTER 6

"Hi," said Norm, walking into the front room to find his mum stretched out on the sofa, phone in one hand and credit card in the other.

"Hello, love," said Norm's mum without taking her eyes off the TV.

Norm turned to see what his mum was watching. An orange lady appeared to be demonstrating how to apply make-up. By the look of things, thought Norm, she'd been applying it for several hours already.

"What did you forget, Mum?" said Norm.

"Sorry, what was that, love?" said Norm's mum absent-mindedly.

"What did you forget?"

"Coffee."

"You want me to get some coffee from the shop?" said Norm.

"No," said Norm's mum. "I want you to get my coffee from the kitchen."

What? thought Norm. Had he heard right?

"Sorry, Mum, did you say from the *kitchen*?"

"That's right," said Norm's mum. "I made it but I

forgot to bring it through."

Norm didn't know quite what to say, but set off for the kitchen anyway. One thing was for sure though. The day wasn't getting any less weird. Or annoying. *Or* unfair.

"What kept you?" said Norm's mum when Norm reappeared a few moments later, holding a mug.

Norm pulled a face. "I'm going as fast as I can, Mum! If I go any faster I'll spill it!"

"No, I mean why did it take you so long to get here after I called, love?"

"Oh, right," said Norm. "I was with Grandpa."

"Where?"

"At the allotments."

"Ah, that would explain it then," said Norm's mum, taking the mug from Norm and *still* not taking her eyes off the TV.

"Explain what, Mum?"

"Why you took so long. I thought you were upstairs."

Norm glanced at the television. The orange lady appeared to be painting eyebrows on her face, giving her a permanently surprised expression. Norm was pretty surprised himself. Even if he **had** been upstairs, what was his mum doing phoning him to fetch her coffee?

"Why couldn't someone else do it?" said Norm.

"No one else is in," said Norm's mum. "They've all gone to the shops."

"Right," said Norm.

Norm's mum took a sip of coffee and screwed up her face. "It's cold."

"What do you flipping expect?" muttered Norm.

"What was that, love?"

"Er, I said I expect it is, Mum," said Norm.

"How was school?"

Norm never quite knew what to say when someone asked him how school was. He never **had** known what to say, and he probably never would. How was school? School was just something you did. Like eating and breathing and going to the toilet. Except at least going to the toilet was vaguely enjoyable.

"It was all right."

"Care to expand on that at all?" said Norm's mum.

"Not really," said Norm.

"My work was fine by the way, thanks for asking," said Norm's mum.

Norm thought for a moment. Was his mum being sarcastic? Because he couldn't actually **remember** asking how her work had been. Then again, Norm had completely forgotten that his mum even **had** a job.

"Oh, yeah. Sorry, Mum."

"Doesn't matter, love. It's not exactly rocket science, is it? Working in a café."

Well of course it wasn't flipping rocket science, thought Norm. Why did people say that? What if you actually **were** a rocket scientist? What would you say then?

"Shhhhh!" said Norm's mum suddenly.

"But I didn't say..." began Norm.

"Shhhhh!" said Norm's mum again, this time even more urgently.

Norm looked at the TV. The orange lady had disappeared – possibly, thought Norm, to let all the make-up dry before applying another coat later on. She'd been replaced by a woman who was holding up what looked to Norm like a perfectly ordinary spoon, to show to the viewers at home.

"It's what I've been waiting for," said Norm's mum. "That's why I didn't want to leave the room."

Norm glanced at his mum for a moment. He'd always assumed that between her and his dad, she was the relatively **normal** one. The relatively **sensible** one. The one with the majority of marbles. But now he was beginning to have his doubts.

"You've been waiting for a spoon, Mum?"

Norm's mum nodded.

"A **spoon**?"

"That's right."

"But we've already **got** spoons," said Norm. "We've got **loads** of spoons."

"Ah, but this isn't just any ordinary spoon," said Norm's mum.

"It's not?" said Norm, looking at the TV again. It looked like any ordinary spoon to him.

"It's slightly smaller than usual," said Norm's mum, as if that somehow explained everything. Which, as far as Norm was concerned, it didn't. "They say if you use smaller cutlery it'll make you eat more slowly."

"But..." said Norm, looking **and** sounding confused.

"But what, love?" said Norm's mum.

"You say that like it's a **good** thing, Mum."

"Eating slowly?" said Norm's mum. "It **is** a good thing."

"Really?" said Norm, looking and sounding even **more** confused. He couldn't for the life of him think how eating more slowly could possibly be a good thing. Eating more slowly meant more time spent away from the computer or, more importantly, his bike. Worse still, eating more slowly meant spending more time sat at the table with his mum and dad and his stupid little brothers. And anyway, thought Norm, surely if you wanted to eat more slowly then you just – well – ate more slowly! Surely you didn't need a special, slightly smaller spoon? And if you did, then why not just use a flipping teaspoon? Whichever way Norm thought about it, it just didn't make sense.

"The slower you eat, the longer it takes to feel full," explained Norm's mum. "Think about it."

Norm thought about it. "Yeah, so?"

"You end up eating less food!"

So *that's* what this was all about, thought Norm. He might have flipping known. Never mind all that stuff about eating slowly! It was all about saving money! Flipping typical!

"Well?" said Norm's mum.

"Well what, Mum?"

"Do you understand?"

"Oh, I understand all right, Mum," said Norm. "I mean it's hardly rocket science, is it?"

Norm's mum looked at Norm. But before she could say anything, the front door burst open and in rushed Dave, Brian and John.

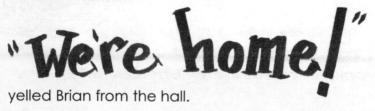

yelled Brian from the hall.

"We know that!" yelled Norm. "We can smell you!"

"Which reminds me," said Norm's mum.

"What?" said Norm.

"You need to clean that mess up."

"What mess?" said Norm.

"The mess next to your bed," said Norm's mum.

"You mean..."

"Exactly."

Norm couldn't believe it. The dog had done a dump next to his bed and **he** was getting the blame? It wasn't even his dog! "But..."

"No buts, love," said Norm's mum. "Now shhhhh! I need to order some of these before they're all gone."

Norm knew that arguing with his mum was about as pointless as having subtitles on the radio. But one thing was for sure, he thought, heading for the stairs. His stupid little brothers were going to have to pay for this.

CHAPTER 7

By the time Norm had cleaned up John's mess and used a can of Dave's deodorant to try and get rid of the smell, his brothers were already sat down and tucking into their tea. Not only that, but to Norm's astonishment it wasn't just **any** old tea.

"Pizza World?" said Norm, appearing in the kitchen doorway and stopping dead in his tracks when he saw the table covered in tell-tale cardboard cartons. Cardboard cartons that **used** to be a familiar sight back in the day but that sadly hadn't been nearly such a familiar sight lately. Not since Norm's dad had been sacked and they'd moved to a smaller house and started eating own-brand Coco Pops, anyway. Norm couldn't remember the last time they'd had a takeaway. What was the occasion? He presumed there **was** one.

"Is it someone's birthday?" said Norm.

"Course it is," said Brian. "It's always *someone's* birthday."

"You know what I mean, Brian, you little freak," spat Norm, sitting down and reaching for a slice of pizza.

"Stop!" said Norm's dad from the fridge, where he was hard at work emptying carrier bags and loading up the freezer compartment.

Norm was confused. "Who, me?"

"Yes you, Norman!" said Norm's dad. "Put that back!"

Now Norm was **_seriously_** confused. "But..."

"I won't tell you again, Norman," said Norm's dad. "Put that pizza back."

Norm grudgingly did as he was told and put the slice of pizza back in the box. This had to be some kind of joke. If so, thought Norm, his dad had just crossed the line. Because there were some things you **_didn't_** joke about. And **_pizza_** was one of them.

"What do you think, boys?" said Norm's dad. "Shall we let him, or not?"

Brian and Dave looked at each other and shrugged.

"Not sure," said Brian.

Norm pulled a face. "What do you mean, you're not sure?"

"He could maybe have a couple of potato wedges," said Dave.

"What?" said Norm.

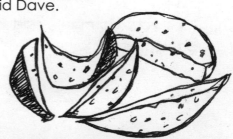

"And a bit of salad."

"Salad?" said Norm, beginning to get more and more exasperated. "Do I **look** like a flipping rabbit?"

"Language," said Dave.

Norm sighed. "Is this for real? Can somebody please tell me what's going on?"

"It's a reward," said Norm's dad.

"What do you mean, 'a reward'?" said Norm.

"Like a prize," said Brian.

Norm sighed again. "I know what a reward is, Brian, you freak! I mean **why** have you been rewarded?"

"Oh, right," said Brian.

"Well?" said Norm.

Brian seemed to hesitate. "Erm…after you, Dave."

"Because I've been good," said Dave.

"And?" said Norm.

"What do you mean 'and'?" said Dave. "That's it."

"That's it?" said Norm. "You've been good?"

Dave nodded.

"We made a deal at the beginning of the week, didn't we, Dave?" said Norm's dad.

Dave nodded again.

"But..." began Norm.

"But what, Norman?" said Norm's dad. "What's the problem?"

What's the problem? thought Norm. Where did he start? How long had his flipping dad got?

"That's **SO** unfair, Dad!" said Norm.

"Do you think so?"

"I don't **think** so. I **know** so!" said Norm.

"Don't answer back, Norman!"

"But..."

"But nothing, Norman!" said Norm's dad. "I said don't answer back!"

Norm sighed.

"And don't sigh like that either."

Norm pulled a face. This was getting ridiculous. First he couldn't answer back. Now he couldn't even flipping sigh. Whatever next?

"And don't pull a face," said Norm's dad, answering Norm's question for him.

Brian sniggered.

"Shut your face, Brian!" snapped Norm. "And anyway, how come you're getting a pizza as well?

Have you been good too?"

Brian seemed to hesitate again. "Erm..."

"What?" said Norm.

"Nothing," said Brian.

Norm looked at his middle brother, but for some reason Brian seemed reluctant to make eye contact.

"Eat up, boys," said Norm's dad. "Ice cream for pudding, remember?"

Norm turned to see his dad holding up a tub of ice cream. Not cheapo supermarket own-brand ice cream either. Proper posh stuff. The real deal. And Norm's favourite flavour too. Mint choc chip.

"Mmmm, yum!" said Brian enthusiastically. A little **too**

enthusiastically actually, thought Norm. Almost as if Brian was trying to change the subject.

Dave suddenly sniffed. "What's that smell?"

"Brian?" said Norm.

Dave sniffed again. "Have you been using my Stynx, Norman?"

"No!" said Norm automatically. Which was true. Or at least partly true. He **hadn't** been using Dave's Stynx. At least not to make **himself** smell better.

"You have!" said Dave. "I can smell it! Dad, Norman's been using my Stynx!"

"Have you?" said Norm's dad.

"Well – yeah, kind of," said Norm. "But only as an air freshener."

"Have you got hormones?" said Dave.

"No, I have **not** got flipping hormones!" said Norm. "It's your flipping dog!"

"John's got hormones?" said Dave.

Norm sighed. "Can I have some pizza, or not?"

"Do you want some?" said Norm's dad.

Norm had heard some stupid questions in his time but that took the biscuit. In fact, never mind the biscuit – it took the whole flipping tin! Did he want some pizza?

"Yes, please," said Norm with as much patience as he could muster.

Norm's dad fixed Norm with a look. "Do you think you **deserve** some pizza?"

"Yes, I do actually, Dad," said Norm. "And a bit of garlic bread if there's some going."

"What do you say, Norman?"

"Er, now?" said Norm hopefully.

Norm's dad raised his eyebrows. Evidently this wasn't quite the answer he'd been looking for.

Norm tried again. "Please?"

"That's better," said Norm's dad. "One slice!"

"One?" said Norm.

"Yes," said Norm's dad. "The one you've touched already."

By now Norm was seething with indignation. One slice of pizza? One measly slice of pizza? That was like...like...like...Norm was seething with **SO** much indignation that he couldn't actually **think** what it was like. But whatever it was like was nothing compared to discovering that there was no more pizza left anyway. Without Norm noticing, someone had already eaten the last slice. And Norm had a pretty good idea who it was, too.

"What?" said Brian innocently.

"What do you mean, **what**?" hissed Norm.

Brian looked confused. "What do you **mean**, what do I mean, **what**?"

Norm sighed. There were two options as far as he could see. He could either stay and get steadily angrier and angrier, **or** he could leave now, go and check Facebook and at least **try** to calm down.

"Something to say?" said Norm's dad as Norm got up from the table.

Something to say? thought Norm. Oh, he'd got something to say all right.

"Two words?" said Norm's dad.

"Excuse me," said Norm, heading for the door.

CHAPTER 8

Before Norm could log onto Facebook, he had to get rid of everything Brian and Dave had been looking at or doing on the PC. He knew that if he didn't, the computer would run even slower than usual. And that was flipping saying something. It was already taking an age to boot up. Sometimes as long as a minute. It was **SO** flipping annoying, thought Norm, deleting a picture of a skateboarding penguin.

Norm sighed. It was times like this when he wished he was an only child, like Mikey. Well, he pretty much **always** wished he was an only child, like Mikey. But it was times like this when he *most* wished he was an only child, like Mikey. Of course, once upon a time he *had* been an only child. But then his parents just *had* to go and ruin everything, didn't they? Some people were just *so* flipping inconsiderate.

The first thing Norm noticed when he eventually logged on was that Mikey was on Facebook too. No doubt on his flipping iPad, thought Norm bitterly. And that was another flipping thing. Had Mikey *really* put money towards it? And if so, how *much* money? It didn't really matter anyway. Mikey got loads of pocket money. So even if he *had* put money towards the iPad, it wasn't actually *his* money in the first flipping place! Yet more proof – if proof was actually needed – that life just wasn't fair. At least not for Norm it wasn't, anyway.

u there norm?
said a message from Mikey.

That was a ridiculous question for a start, thought Norm. Of *course* he was there! Where else would he be? And anyway, Mikey would have seen the green dot next to Norm's name on the screen. There was no need to ask. He *knew* he was there!

yeah
typed Norm.

alrite?
said another message from Mikey a moment later.

What *is* this? thought Norm. Ask one ridiculous question, ask another one free? Of *course* he wasn't all right. He was anything *but* all right!

yeah
typed Norm again.

gud
said Mikey.
thort u wer cros.

nah
typed Norm.

Which was *kind* of true. Norm *wasn't* cross. He was

livid! But he wasn't going to tell Mikey that. He didn't want to give Mikey the satisfaction of knowing that he was completely consumed with jealousy. Although, knowing Mikey as Norm did, Mikey wouldn't get *any* satisfaction from knowing Norm was jealous because he was just too flipping nice!

Norm heard the tell-tale creak of the creaky floorboard. This could only mean one of two things. Either the house was haunted or, more likely, there was somebody there.

"Who is it?" said Norm, without bothering to turn around.

CREAK!

"Me," said Dave.

"What do you want?"

"Nothing," said Dave.

"Clear off then," said Norm. "Can't you see I'm busy here?"

"What you doing?"

"Stuff."

"What kind of stuff?"

Norm sighed. "Stuff kind of stuff."

"Stuff kind of stuff?" said Dave.

Norm nodded. "Now clear off."

"'Kay," said Dave, turning to leave.

Norm had a sudden thought. "Actually, Dave."

Dave stopped. "What?"

Norm spun round so that he could give his little brother the benefit of his full attention. "You might be able to help me."

"Oh, yeah?" said Dave.

"Yeah," said Norm.

Norm eyeballed Dave for a moment. For a seven-year-old, Dave was a pretty smart cookie. Norm knew that. Dave knew that. Dave knew that Norm knew that. Norm knew that Dave knew that Norm knew that.

"It'll cost you," said Dave.

Norm pulled a face. "But you don't know what I'm going to ask you yet."

"Two cans of Stynx," said Dave.

"What?" said Norm.

"You heard," said Dave. "Two cans of Stynx."

Norm thought for a moment. That was fair enough. He'd used the best part of a can to try and get rid of the smell in his room earlier.

"Deal?" said Dave.

"Deal," said Norm.

Dave shrugged. "Well?"

"Well what?"

"What do you want to know?" said Dave.

"What did Brian actually do to earn his so-called 'reward'?" said Norm, making quote signs in the air with his fingers.

Dave laughed. "What **didn't** he do, more like."

"What do you mean?" said Norm.

Dave hesitated. "I'm not sure I should say."

"Go on, Dave."

"Three cans."

"What?" said Norm.

"Three cans of Stynx," said Dave.

Norm sighed. "OK. Three cans."

Dave hesitated again. "He didn't wet his bed for a week."

Norm grinned. "Are you serious?"

"You mustn't say anything, Norman!"

"As if," said Norm.

"Promise?" said Dave.

"Promise," said Norm.

"Dave?" called Norm's mum from the foot of the stairs.

Dave glared at Norm.

"What?" said Norm. "I said I won't say anything!"

"Coming, Mum!" called Dave, hurrying off.

Norm watched him go, his mind already whirring into action. Dave had nothing to worry about. Norm wouldn't actually *say* anything. Didn't mean he couldn't update his Facebook status though, did it?

CHAPTER 9

The next day being Saturday, Norm was out on the drive straight after breakfast, fiddling about with his bike. A good night's sleep hadn't done anything to improve his mood, but at least he hadn't trodden on Brian – or anything else for that matter – when he'd got out of bed that morning. And at least he hadn't woken up to find Dave sleeping next to him. No, thought Norm, things could be worse. And pretty soon they were.

"Hello, **Norman!**" said an all too familiar voice, in an all too familiar, mocking kind of way.

Gordon flipping Bennet, thought Norm. Why did Chelsea always have to show up just when he least wanted her to. Not that Norm ever actually **wanted** Chelsea to show up. At all. Let alone when he **least** wanted her to.

"What's the matter, **Norman**?" said Chelsea when Norm didn't reply. "Cat got your tongue?"

"Wish it'd got yours," muttered Norm under his breath.

"What was that?" said Chelsea.

"Nothing," said Norm without looking up.

Chelsea eyed Norm from the other side of the fence, which as far as Norm was concerned was the best place for her. It was certainly better than eyeing him from **his** side of the fence. But only marginally.

"What are you doing?" said Chelsea.

"Playing on the Xbox," said Norm.

"No, but really?" said Chelsea.

Norm sighed. He might as well just answer her and get it over with. The sooner he got it over with, the sooner she'd go. With any luck.

"Pimping my bike," said Norm.

"*Pimping it*?" said Chelsea.

Norm nodded. "Yeah. Just, kind of – you know?"

"No, I *don't* know, **Norman**," said Chelsea. "I don't speak Geek."

Norm sighed again. What was it about Chelsea that he found so annoying? Oh yeah, thought Norm. That was it. Everything. Just as well she only lived next door with her dad at weekends. It was still two days a week too many though, as far as Norm was concerned.

"I'm adjusting the front fork suspension if you must know," said Norm. "Making it softer. Better for going over rocks and roots and jumping off steps and stuff."

"Wow!" said Chelsea sarcastically. "That's really fascinating!"

Norm – something of an expert himself when it came to sarcasm – didn't fall for it. "Yeah, yeah. Very funny."

"What?" said Chelsea. "No, really. I mean it. It sounds fascinating."

Norm turned round and looked at Chelsea. "Really?"

Chelsea held Norm's gaze for a couple of seconds before bursting out laughing.

"I knew you weren't being serious," said Norm.

"Yeah, right," said Chelsea.

Norm turned back to his bike, silently fuming. Chelsea had got one over on him and they both knew it. It was **SO** flipping annoying.

"So, how are you?" said Chelsea.

"Busy," mumbled Norm.

But Chelsea wasn't easily put off. "That's OK. I can soon find out."

Uh? thought Norm, turning round again to find Chelsea tapping away on a suspiciously tablet-shaped portable computer.

"What is it, **Norman**? You look like you've never *seen* an iPad before!"

Norm shrugged as nonchalantly as he could. "I've seen one before. I've seen plenty before."

"What?" grinned Chelsea. "You mean in your dreams?"

Norm was so gobsmacked he couldn't even think of a suitable witty comeback. All Norm could think of was the fact that he appeared to be the only kid on the planet who **didn't** have an iPad.

"So Brian's a bed-wetter, is he?" said Chelsea.

"How do you know that?" said Norm.

"It says here," said Chelsea. "'One brother's a bed-wetter and the other one's called Dave.'"

Norm suddenly twigged. "Get off my Facebook!"

Chelsea laughed. "Let me think about that for a moment, **Norman**. Right. Thought about it. No."

"What do you mean, 'no'?" said Norm. "Only my friends can see that!"

"How **is** Mikey, anyway?" said Chelsea.

That was it. Norm felt like a firework ready to explode. And Chelsea had just lit the match! How flipping **dare** she look at his Facebook? How flipping **dare** she imply that he'd only got one friend? And how flipping **dare** she have a flipping iPad?

"Give it here!" said Norm, standing up and marching towards the fence, one hand outstretched.

"What?" said Chelsea.

"You heard," said Norm.

"You're not serious, are you?" said Chelsea. "You don't honestly expect me to hand over this brand-new, top-of-the-range, state-of-the-art, hand-held tablet computer just like that?"

Norm thought for a moment. Chelsea had got a point. He *didn't* really expect her to hand the iPad over just like that. What was he thinking? But what was he supposed to do now? Back down, or just stand there with his hand stuck out like a complete doughnut?

"If you don't want people looking at your Facebook, you need to change your privacy settings, *Norman*!"

"Yeah, well…" began Norm.

"Yeah, well, nothing," said Chelsea.

"Nice," said a voice.

Norm spun round to see Grandpa walking up the drive. Not only that, but he appeared to be making a beeline for Chelsea.

"Is that the latest one?"

"Yeah," said Chelsea.

"Thirty-two gigabyte?" said Grandpa.

"Sixty-four," said Chelsea.

"Facetime camera?"

"Naturally."

Grandpa nodded approvingly. "Very nice."

"Thanks," said Chelsea.

"I might have to upgrade," said Grandpa.

"Cool," said Chelsea.

Norm didn't say anything. Norm **couldn't** say anything. Was this for real, or some kind of sick joke? His **grandpa** had an iPad? Grandpas were supposed to have hair sprouting out of their ears and an addiction to Extra Strong Mints – not flipping iPads!

"Morning, Norman, by the way," said Grandpa.

"Hi," Norm just about managed to croak.

"Norman?" called Norm's mum from an open upstairs window.

"Yeah?" said Norm, looking up.

"Can I see you?"

Norm shrugged. "I dunno, Mum. Can you?"

"I mean, can I see you upstairs, please? Now?"

Under normal circumstances, Norm would have been a bit embarrassed to be called inside by his mum in front of Chelsea. Not today though. Norm was only too glad to be called inside. Even if he had no idea what lay in store for him.

"Coming, Mum," said Norm, heading for the door.

"Good boy," chuckled Chelsea, watching him go.

CHAPTER 10

Norm walked into his bedroom to find his mum holding a letter. Not just any old letter either. The letter from his maths teacher, Mrs Simpson.

Oops, thought Norm.

"What do you call this?" said Norm's mum, cutting straight to the chase.

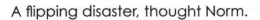

A flipping disaster, thought Norm.

"Something you'd like to say to me?" said Norm's mum.

"Yeah," said Norm. "Where did you find it, Mum?"

"It doesn't matter **who** showed it to me."

Norm looked at his mum. "What?"

"I mean, where I found it," said Norm's mum quickly.

But it was too late. The damage had already been done. Norm's mum had just made a big mistake and they both knew it. Norm had obviously been grassed up by one of his brothers. The question was – which one?

"Don't you **dare** do anything to him, Norman!"

"Do anything to who?" said Norm.

"Dave," said Norm's mum.

Norm's mum had just made her second big mistake and they both knew it. But at least it took the guesswork out of it, thought Norm. He'd kind of assumed it was Brian just because... just because...Well, just because, basically. But it now appeared that he was wrong.

"It makes no difference **who** showed it to me," said Norm's mum. "That's not the point."

"I think you'll find it is," muttered Norm.

"Pardon?" said Norm's mum.

"Nothing," said Norm.

"Your father's not going to be very happy about this when I tell him," said Norm's mum.

"**When** you tell him, Mum?" said Norm, immediately sensing an opportunity for negotiation. "Or **if** you tell him?"

"What do you mean?"

Norm shrugged. "Dunno, Mum. I was just wondering, that's all."

Norm's mum raised her eyebrows.

"You got any jobs need doing?"

"Are you serious?" said Norm's mum.

Norm thought for a moment. Course he was flipping serious. Why wouldn't he be?

"You honestly expect me **not** to tell your dad about this if you do the washing up or something?"

Norm nodded. "Basically, yeah. But it doesn't necessarily need to be the washing up. Could be... emptying the bins? Bit of hoovering? Whatever really. The choice is yours, Mum."

"Unbelievable," said Norm's mum.

"Excellent," said Norm. "What's it to be then?"

Norm's mum looked at Norm. "Not unbelievable as in 'thanks very much'."

Uh? thought Norm.

"Unbelievable as in 'you've got some nerve'."

It took a moment for the penny to drop. But it finally dropped.

"Oh, I see," said Norm. "But..."

"But what?" said Norm's mum.

"It's no big deal, Mum."

"No big deal?"

"It's only a letter."

"It's a letter of **_concern_**!" said Norm's mum. "**_Concern!_**"

"Heard you the first time," muttered Norm.

"Pardon?"

"Nothing," said Norm.

"Have there been any others?"

"Other letters?" said Norm. "Of concern, you mean?"

Norm's mum nodded.

"Loads," said Norm.

Norm's mum looked absolutely horrified. "What?"

"Loads of other people have had them," said Norm. "Happens all the time!"

Norm's mum exhaled loudly.

"What?" said Norm.

"I meant, have **you** had any others?"

"What?" said Norm. "Oh, right! I see what you mean, Mum."

"And?" said Norm's mum expectantly.

Norm shook his head. "It's my first one."

Norm's mum gave Norm a look.

"What?" said Norm. "It **is**!"

"Promise?"

"Promise," said Norm.

"Thank goodness for that!" said Norm's mum.

"Well, I'm glad we got that cleared up," said Norm, heading for the door. "Now if you'll excuse me..."

"Where do you think you're going?" said Norm's mum. "Get back in here!"

Norm turned round again. "But..."

"But what?" said Norm's mum. "You don't honestly think you're going to get away with it *that* easily, do you?"

"Erm, well, actually..." began Norm.

"What's wrong, love?" said Norm's mum, adopting a gentler and altogether more sympathetic tone. "Is there a problem?"

Is there a problem? thought Norm. Yes, there was a flipping problem. He was supposed to be pimping his bike up and then going for a ride!

"You can tell me," said Norm's mum. "I'm your mother."

Brilliant, thought Norm. Thanks for clearing *that* up.

"Come here," said Norm's mum, sitting down on Norm's bed and patting the space beside her.

Norm sighed. He knew what this meant. It meant his mum wanted to have a flipping heart-to-heart chat and talk about his flipping feelings and stuff. And frankly, thought Norm, he'd got better things to do than talk about his flipping feelings. Like... like...well, like just about anything. Life was too short to talk about flipping feelings. Feelings were what grown-ups had. And geeks. And girls.

"Let's talk," said Norm's mum.

Let's not, thought Norm.

"After you," said Norm's mum.

"No really, Mum. I insist," said Norm. "After you."

Norm's mum smiled. Or at least **tried** to. "Why, love?"

Norm shrugged. "I was just being polite."

"What?" said Norm's mum. "No, I meant **why** did you get a letter?"

Norm shrugged again. "'Cos I didn't do my homework."

"I know that, love," said Norm's mum patiently. "But **why** didn't you do it? That's what I want to know."

Norm thought for a moment. What was that thing Mrs Simpson had said again?

"I thought it was rhetorical."

"Pardon?" said Norm's mum.

"I thought the homework was rhetorical," said Norm. "I didn't think you had to do it if you didn't want to."

Norm actually felt quite pleased with himself. It sounded perfectly reasonable. He'd even managed to use a big word. So much for kids today having no imagination. Not only should his mum **not** be cross with him – he should get the rest of the flipping day off.

"No, but really, love," said Norm's mum.

Norm sighed. So much for that, then. His mum clearly wasn't having any of it.

"Well?" said Norm's mum.

"Forgot," mumbled Norm.

"You forgot to do your homework?" said Norm's mum.

"No," said Norm. "I've forgotten why I didn't do it."

Norm's mum smiled again. Or at least **tried** to smile again.

"What?" said Norm indignantly.

"You can do better than that, love."

His mum was right, thought Norm. He flipping could. He flipping would.

"I needed the computer."

"To do your homework?" said Norm's mum.

"Yeah," said Norm.

"Your maths homework?"

"Yeah," said Norm.

"Hmm," said Norm's mum.

Hmm? thought Norm. What was 'hmm' supposed to flipping mean? Did his mum not believe him or something? OK, so as it happened, he *had* just made it up on the spur of the moment. He hadn't needed a computer to do his homework any more than he'd needed a flipping stepladder. But that was hardly the point. The point was...The point was...Actually, Norm couldn't think what the point was. But that wasn't the point either.

"So, then what?" said Norm's mum expectantly.

It was a very good question, thought Norm. Then what? This clearly required a bit more creative thinking.

"It's obvious, isn't it?"

Norm's mum pulled a face. Seemingly, whatever it was that Norm thought was obvious wasn't *quite* as obvious as he'd thought.

"It's a rubbish computer!" said Norm.

"Oh, I see," said Norm's mum. "So the reason you didn't do your homework was because the computer's rubbish?"

"Yeah," said Norm. "It's really slow and it's always crashing."

"Right," said Norm's mum.

"Either that or my stupid brothers are on it."

"Why shouldn't they be, love? It's theirs as well."

"It's **SO** unfair!"

"What is?"

"Only having one computer in the house!" said Norm. "It's ridiculous!"

Norm's mum laughed. "Have you any idea what you're saying?"

Norm looked at his mum. This just **had** to be a rhetorical question! He knew **exactly** what he was saying!

"When I was your age we didn't have **any** computers in the house!" said Norm's mum. "Never mind more than **one**!"

Norm didn't know where to start. When his mum was **his** age? That was like three hundred years ago or something! Flipping dinosaurs had only just died out!

"I need an iPad, Mum!"

Norm's mum looked at Norm. "Ah! So *that's* what this is about!"

Norm thought for a moment. Now his mum came to mention it, that was *exactly* what this was about.

"Need or want?"

"What?" said Norm.

"Do you *need* an iPad? Or *want* an iPad? There's a big difference."

There is? thought Norm.

"Everybody's got one, Mum!"

Norm's mum raised her eyebrows. "Everybody?"

"Yeah."

"Who's everybody?"

"Mikey," said Norm. "And Chelsea. And Grandpa."

"Grandpa?"

Norm nodded.

"That's three people."

"Yeah, well,"
said Norm.

"What's so good
about iPads?" said Norm's mum.

Once again, Norm scarcely knew where to start.
What was so good about iPads? That was like
asking what was so good about breathing!

"You get apps."

"Apps?" said Norm's mum.

"Yeah," said Norm. "They're like these things you
download from the—"

"I know what apps are, love."

"Really?" said Norm.

"I'm not quite as daft as I look," said Norm's mum.

"Not **quite**," muttered Norm.

"What was that, love?"

"Nothing, Mum."

"Anyone home?" called Grandpa from the bottom of the stairs.

"Be down in a minute, Dad!" called Norm's mum. "Make yourself a cup of tea!"

"Already have!" called Grandpa.

Norm could see the opportunity beginning to pass him by. What little opportunity there was.

"Can we talk about this later, Mum?"

Norm's mum pulled a face. "If you want to."

Norm nodded. He wanted to all right. He abso-flipping-lutely wanted to.

CHAPTER 11

"Well, you're a bit of a dark horse, aren't you?" said Norm's mum, sitting down at the kitchen table.

Grandpa took a slurp of his tea.
"What do you mean?"

"I didn't know you had an iPad!"

Grandpa's eyes crinkled ever so slightly in the corners. "Oh, there's a lot you don't know about me."

Norm's mum pulled a face.
"Really, Dad? Like what?"

"Can't possibly tell you," said Grandpa mysteriously.

"Oh?" said Norm's mum. "And why not?"

"I don't know what it is yet," said Grandpa.

Uh? thought Norm, watching from the doorway. What on earth were his mum and grandpa on about? He was used to his little brothers spouting gibberish. But this was taking gibberish to a whole new level. This was like watching two different movies at once. In two different languages.

Grandpa took another slurp of his tea before carrying on. "That's why I wanted an iPad."

"Oh yeah?" said Norm's mum.

"It's got a whatsit," said Grandpa.

"A whatsit?" said Norm's mum.

"A thingy," said Grandpa.

"An app?" said Norm.

"An app. That's it," said Grandpa. "For discovering your family tree."

Norm thought for a moment. They had a family

tree? First he knew of it. "So you mean we've got, like, ancestors and stuff?"

"Everybody's got ancestors, love," laughed Norm's mum.

"But..."

"We've all got to come from somewhere!"

"Aaaaagh!" said Norm. "That is so **gross**, Mum!"

"That's not what I meant," said Norm's mum. "I meant, we all have a past. We all have history."

"Even you, Norman," said Grandpa.

"I hate history," mumbled Norm. "All those kings and queens and stuff. It's well boring."

Grandpa's eyes crinkled in the corners again. "History's not all about kings and queens, you know."

Norm shrugged. "Whatever."

"You never know," said Grandpa. "You might be related to someone famous."

Norm looked at Grandpa. "Really?"

"Probably not," said Grandpa. "But that's what I'm trying to find out."

"How far have you got?" said Norm's mum.

"I've taken it out of the box," said Grandpa.

Norm's mum laughed. "Well, that's a start, I suppose."

Norm sighed.

"What's up?" said Grandpa.

"He wants one as well," said Norm's mum.

"An iPad?" said Grandpa. "Yes, so he was saying."

"It's not going to happen though, I'm afraid," said Norm's mum.

"But…" said Norm.

"But what, love?"

"That is **SO** unfair, Mum!"

"Really?" said Norm's mum. "You honestly think **that's** unfair?"

Norm thought for a moment. "Yeah, Mum. I honestly do."

"Think about it."

"Just did," muttered Norm. "Still unfair."

Norm's mum took a deep breath and let it back out slowly. "Why?"

"Why what?" said Norm.

"Why do you think it's unfair?"

Norm looked at his mum. Of all the dumb questions so far, that had to be the dumbest. Why was it unfair? Wasn't it screamingly obvious?

"Well?" said Norm's mum.

"Brian and Dave got a pizza!"

Norm's mum and Grandpa exchanged a quick look. "So you think you should get an iPad?"

Norm shrugged. "Yeah. Why not?"

"It was a pizza! That's why not!" said Norm's mum. "A pizza!"

"Yeah but it was an eighteen-inch deep-crust pepperoni," said Norm. "**And** they had potato wedges!"

"Good point," said Norm's mum. "I'd forgotten about the potato wedges. Well, that changes everything."

"Really?" said Norm hopefully.

"No, love. Not really."

Norm sighed.

"Your brothers were bought a pizza as a **reward**," said Norm's mum.

Yeah, thought Norm. A reward for **not** doing something. In Dave's case, **not** misbehaving and in Brian's, **not** wetting the flipping bed! They hadn't actually **done** anything!

"Tell me why you think **you** should be rewarded, love."

Norm pulled a face. "Not getting another letter?"

Norm's mum was gobsmacked. "Are you serious?"

"OK," said Norm. "How about not getting another two letters?"

Norm's mum shook her head in disbelief.

"My final offer," said Norm. "Not getting another **five** letters."

"Is someone going to tell me what you're talking about, or do I have to guess?" said Grandpa.

"He got a letter of concern from school, Dad," said Norm's mum.

"Oh, did he now?" said Grandpa. "What for?"

"For not doing his homework."

"I would've done if I'd had a flipping iPad!" said Norm.

"Language," said Norm's mum.

Grandpa looked at Norm. "Would you *really* have done it if you'd had an iPad?"

Norm shrugged. "Dunno. Probably. It's not the end of the world, Grandpa. It's only homework!"

"Well, you say that," said Grandpa.

"What do you mean, Grandpa?" said Norm.

Grandpa scratched his head. "I have no idea."

Norm laughed. He couldn't help it.

"I know what it's like to want something, love," said Norm's mum gently.

"Like spoons?" said Norm.

"Exactly," said Norm's mum.

Grandpa looked confused. "Spoons?"

Norm's mum nodded. "Small spoons. To stop me eating so much."

Grandpa turned to Norm and shrugged.

"Me neither," said Norm.

"You know, you could always save up," said Grandpa.

The kitchen suddenly went very quiet. Even the fridge seemed to stop humming for a few moments.

"Sorry, were you talking to me, Grandpa?" said Norm, finally realising that no one else was saying anything.

"I said you could always save up," said Grandpa.

"What?" said Norm.
"You mean like – money?"

"No. Cheese," said Grandpa.

"Uh?" said Norm. "Cheese?"

"Of course I mean money."

Norm was temporarily speechless. As if someone had just pointed a remote control at him and hit the mute button. Even if he **had** been able to say something, it was very doubtful whether he would have been able to actually **think** of something to say. Save money? Grandpa might as well have suggested listening to opera, or talking to squid. It was a completely alien concept to Norm. One which he'd never totally managed to get his head round. Or even partially.

"Well?" said Grandpa.

Norm looked closely at Grandpa, waiting for the tell-tale crinkling of the eyes in the corners. But Grandpa's eyes remained a resolutely crinkle-free zone. This could only mean one thing, thought Norm. Grandpa wasn't joking. He really did seem to be suggesting that Norm saved up money in order to buy an iPad.

"How?" said Norm.

"No idea," said Grandpa.

That's flipping useful then, isn't it? thought Norm.

"You get pocket money, don't you?"

"Sometimes," said Norm, glancing meaningfully at his mum. "It would take forever to save up enough for an iPad though!"

Actually, thought Norm, it would take longer than that, the measly amount of pocket money he got from his stingy parents. Or occasionally got, anyway. By the time he'd saved up for an iPad, the only place you'd actually be able to **see** an iPad would be in a flipping museum, they'd be so out of date! There'd be no need for anyone to actually **own** a computer by then because everyone would get a flipping microchip injected into their bum when they were born or something. And anyway, they'd all be living on the flipping planet Zarg so who flipping cared?

"You could always sell your bike."

Norm looked at Grandpa as if Grandpa had just told him to strip down to his pants, smear his body in baked beans and run through the shopping precinct. Sell his bike? He'd **thought** about it briefly the day before. But actually do it? There was more chance of Norm selling

Dave than there was of him selling his bike! Especially since it had been Dave who'd snitched on him about the letter in the first place!

"No, but really, Grandpa."

"What?" said Grandpa. "I'm serious."

"There's no way I'm selling my bike!"

Grandpa shrugged his shoulders. "So get a job then."

"What?" said Norm.

"***Earn*** the money."

Norm furrowed his brow until his eyebrows almost met in the middle. Job? Earn? This was another alien concept.

"You work? You get paid," said Grandpa. "You don't work? You don't get paid. It's not exactly rocket science."

Norm didn't say anything.

"What are you thinking?" said Grandpa.

"What?" said Norm. "Oh, nothing, Grandpa. I was just wondering how much rocket scientists get paid."

"Talking about earning money," said Norm's mum, getting up from the table and heading for the doorway, where Norm was still standing. "Excuse me, love."

"Uh?" said Norm.

"I need to get past," said Norm's mum. "I'm late

for work. Put the mugs in the dishwasher for me, would you?"

Norm pulled a face. "We've got a dishwasher?"

"Just do it please, love."

"How much?" said Norm.

Norm's mum stopped. "Sorry, what was that?"

"How much?" said Norm.

"For putting two mugs in the dishwasher?" said Norm's mum.

"Yeah," said Norm. "How does a pound sound?"

"Incredible," said Norm's mum, shaking her head in disbelief.

"Excellent," said Norm. "That's a deal then."

But it was too late. There was a clanking of crockery. Norm turned round to see Grandpa already loading up the dishwasher.

CHAPTER 12

Norm hadn't actually **meant** to bump into Mikey whilst he was out and about on his bike, but it wasn't exactly a major surprise when he **did**. It wasn't as if they lived in a huge city. Or even a medium-sized city. It was only a small town. And there were only a certain number of places that were any good for biking. Unfortunately – as far as Norm was concerned anyway – school just happened to be one of them. But that was OK. It was a Saturday. There was actually something pretty cool about whizzing round the playground when no one else was there. It felt just a little bit wrong. A little bit naughty. Like going to school for parents' evening and not having to wear uniform.

"Hi," said Mikey, skidding to a halt next to the science block, where Norm was busy concentrating, balancing along a low wall.

Norm wobbled alarmingly and very nearly fell off his bike **and** the wall. "What are you doing here, Mikey?"

Mikey was unsure what to say. He knew that he was perfectly entitled to be there. Norm knew that Mikey knew that, too. Mikey also knew that Norm knew that Mikey knew that. But things were still a bit awkward – as they had been ever since Norm had discovered that Mikey had an iPad.

"Just, you know…" began Mikey, before trailing off into silence.

"Yeah," said Norm.

The two friends looked at each other for a moment.

"Sorry, Mikey," said Norm.

Mikey shrugged as if he hadn't got the faintest idea what Norm was on about. "What for?"

"For being a doughnut," said Norm. "You know, about the iPad?"

"Oh, *that*," said Mikey. "That's OK. I'm sorry if I... well...you know..."

"You don't need to explain," said Norm.

Mikey looked visibly relieved.

"You can probably get an app to do it for you."

"What?" said Mikey, concern written all over his face.

Norm waited a second before allowing himself a slight smile. "I'm just kidding, Mikey. Honest."

"So are we....?"

"What?" said Norm. "Cool?"

Mikey nodded.

"Course we're flipping cool, Mikey, you flipping doughnut!"

Mikey puffed his cheeks out and released the lungful of air he'd been holding in.

"Can I ask you a question though?" said Norm.

"Go for it," said Mikey.

"You know the money you put towards it?"

"Yeah?" said Mikey.

"Where d'ya get it from?"

Mikey shrugged. "I earned it."

Norm pulled a face. This was a bit unexpected. Actually this was more than a *bit* unexpected. This was *very* unexpected. Mikey had *earned* it? Actually *earned* it?

"What? All of it?" said Norm.

"A fair bit of it," said Mikey.

"Whoa," said Norm. "How?"

Mikey suddenly looked uncomfortable. As if he didn't really want to **say** how.

"Erm…"

"Well?" said Norm.

"Working for my dad," mumbled Mikey.

Right, thought Norm. So **that** was why Mikey had hesitated. Out of **consideration**. Consideration of the fact that **his** dad actually **had** a job – but Norm's dad didn't. Mikey really didn't have a single bad atom in his entire body. It was **so** flipping annoying!

"What does your dad actually do?" said Norm.

Mikey couldn't help laughing. "How long have we known each other, Norm?"

Norm didn't see what that had to do with anything. How long had he and Mikey known each other? Who flipping cared? There were some things you just didn't ever talk about. The price of fish was one of them. What jobs parents had was another. Norm didn't  even know what his **own** dad did – let alone what **other** dads did!

Of course, these days Norm's dad didn't do anything as far as Norm could tell, apart from going round the house switching lights off and turning radiators down. Not since he'd got sacked from whatever job he'd had. But that wasn't the point, thought Norm, forgetting what the point had been in the first place.

"He's in IT," said Mikey.

"Right," said Norm, none the wiser.

"Software engineer."

Norm was still none the wiser. But he wanted to know. Well, he didn't exactly **want** to know. But he kind of **needed** to know. It was beginning to look more and more as if Grandpa might actually be right. Unless scientists somewhere suddenly discovered that money **did** in fact grow on trees after all, Norm faced the frankly horrific prospect of actually having to **earn** money himself if there was the remotest chance of him ever getting an iPad.

"So what do you actually do for him, then?" said Norm.

"CEO," said Mikey.

Uh? thought Norm. And what did **that** mean when it was at home? CEO? That was just three random letters strung together. Mikey might as well have said that he was an OMG or a flipping LOL!

"Head of advertising, basically," said Mikey.

"Advertising?" said Norm.

"Delivering leaflets," said Mikey.

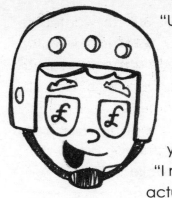

"Uh?" said Norm. "What for?"

Mikey pulled a face. "Money!"

"Yeah, I know that, Mikey, you doughnut," said Norm. "I mean, what are the leaflets actually for?"

"Oh, right," said Mikey. "Dad's setting up his own business."

"What kind of business?"

"Repairs and upgrades for laptops and stuff."

"Stuff?" said Norm.

Mikey hesitated slightly. "iPads?"

"Right," said Norm.

"He's just trying to get things off the ground really," said Mikey. "Word of mouth and all that."

"Yeah," said Norm.

"He says he wants me to set up a Facebook page and a Twitter account too."

"Cool," said Norm.

"So what with that and the pocket money..."

"Yeah, yeah," said Norm. "No, that's great."

They looked at each other for a moment.

"I could ask him if maybe you could..."

"What?" said Norm. "Nah, nah, you're all right thanks, Mikey."

It was nice of Mikey to offer, thought Norm. But actually the last thing he wanted was charity. Actually, thought Norm, that wasn't strictly true. The *last* thing he wanted was broccoli. But charity was right up there near the top of the

WANTS
1. iPAD!
£££
NEW BiKe
PIZZA
CHARITY
BROCCOLI

list too. Or the bottom of the list depending on which way you looked at it.

"Anyway," said Mikey.

"Yeah," said Norm.

"Better go," said Mikey.

"Yeah, me too," said Norm.

"Things to do," said Mikey.

Norm nodded. "Me too."

They cycled out through the school gates together – Norm turning one way and Mikey the other. Norm had no idea about precisely what **kind** of things he had to do. One thing was for sure though. Working for his dad wasn't one of the options. Not unless his dad paid him every time he switched a flipping light off.

CHAPTER 13

It was almost lunchtime when Norm got home to find Dave kicking a ball against the garage door.

"I want a word with you," said Norm, pedalling up the drive.

"Funny you should say that," said Dave, without bothering to turn round.

"Is it?" said Norm. "Why's that, then?"

"I want one with you as well," said Dave.

Norm pulled a face. What did Dave want a word with **him** about?

"Go on, then."

"After you," said Dave.

Norm looked at his little brother. It was weird. He really should be mad at him for showing his mum the letter. **Seriously** mad. But in a roundabout kind of way, Dave had actually done him a favour. Because if Dave hadn't shown his mum the letter from school, Norm wouldn't have had the discussion with his mum about not doing his homework. And if Norm hadn't had the discussion with his mum about not doing his homework, the subject of rubbish computers and iPads might never have cropped up. And if...

"Well?" said Dave, derailing Norm's train of thought.

"What?" said Norm.

"What do you want a word with me about?"

"Oh right," said Norm. "Why did you have to go and show Mum that letter?"

Dave finally turned round. "I didn't have to."

"What?" said Norm.

"I didn't **have** to," said Dave. "I **chose** to."

Norm sighed. He wasn't in the mood for this. "Whatever."

"Let me ask YOU a question," said Dave.

Gordon flipping Bennet, thought Norm. It was beginning to feel as if he was in some kind of flipping TV drama or something! Surely people didn't **really** talk like this?

"What are you on about, Dave?"

"Why did you do it?"

Norm thought for a moment. Why did he do **what**? If Dave didn't hurry up and spit it out soon it'd be time for a flipping ad break!

"You promised," said Dave.

"Promised **what**?!" yelled Norm. "Stop talking in flipping riddles will you, Dave?!"

Dave looked round to make sure they weren't being overheard.

"Not to say anything about...you know?"

Norm sighed. "No, Dave. I **don't** know!"

"Brian **thingying** the bed," whispered Dave.

"**Thingying** the bed?" said Norm. "Oh right! You mean we—"

"*Shhhhhh!*" said Dave, eyes blazing furiously. "We don't want the whole street to know!"

Norm chuckled. "Don't we?"

"He can't help it," said Dave. "Mum and Dad reckon that subconsciously Brian's still upset about moving house."

Norm snorted derisively. "Tell me about it!"

"I heard them," said Dave. "They said he hasn't quite been the same ever since."

"Dave?"

"Yeah?"

"I didn't **really** mean tell me about it."

"Oh," said Dave.

So Brian hadn't been the same ever since they'd moved, eh? thought Norm. Well, boo flipping hoo. **He** hadn't been the same ever since Brian had been flipping born!

"You still owe me three cans of Stynx, by the way," said Dave.

"Yeah, well, I haven't got any, have I?"

"I know," said Dave.

"**How** do you know?"

"I looked."

"What?" said Norm.

Dave shrugged. "I looked."

Norm could feel himself beginning to boil up inside. "You were in my room?"

"Yeah, well, technically it's not **your** room, is it?" said Dave. "You don't actually **own** it."

Norm took a deep breath. It was pointless trying to argue with Dave. Dave was right. And when Dave was right, the rest of the world was wrong. End of.

"So that's how you found the letter, then?"

Dave shrugged. "Might be."

"Might be what?" said Chelsea, suddenly appearing on the other side of the fence.

"Time you minded your own flipping business," muttered Norm.

"Oooooooh!" said Chelsea sarcastically. "Bit touchy aren't we, **Norman**?"

"We're actually in the middle of a private conversation here, in case you haven't noticed," said Norm.

"What about?" said Chelsea.

Unbe-flipping-lievable, thought Norm. Which part of **private** did she not flipping understand? Did **everybody** find Chelsea this annoying – or was it just **him**? It was as if she was on some kind of personal mission to make his life as miserable as possible. As if Norm was some kind of personal project of hers.

"Let me guess," said Chelsea, smiling sweetly. "You

were talking about me, weren't you, **Norman**?"

"No we flipping weren't!"
said Norm.

"All right, all right," said
Chelsea. "Keep your
hair on, **Norman!**"

Dave giggled.

"Shut up, Dave!" hissed Norm.

"I see you've changed your Facebook profile, by
the way," said Chelsea.

It was only now that Norm noticed Chelsea had
her iPad with her, and that she appeared to be
browsing whilst talking to him. Unless she was just
pretending, to try and wind him up even **more**.

"I didn't change it," said Norm.

"Really?" said Chelsea.

"It was me," said Dave. "I did it."

Norm turned to Dave. "You've been on my Facebook?"

Dave shrugged. "Yeah? So?"

Norm pulled a face. "So you **shouldn't** have been!"

"You shouldn't have written that about Brian!" said Dave. "That was confidential!"

"That is **SO** sweet!" said Chelsea.

"Are you still here?" said Norm, turning back to Chelsea.

"Good question," said Chelsea. "Am I still here? I'll just Google it and find out."

Norm decided to ignore Chelsea and concentrate instead on how exactly his Facebook page had been hacked into in the first place.

"How d'ya know what my password is, Dave?"

Dave shrugged again. "I just typed in 'Password'. Turns out that's your password."

Norm sighed.

"It's not exactly rocket science," said Dave.

"Dave?" said Norm.

"What?" said Dave.

"Shut up."

CHAPTER 14

"Ah, good, there you are, Norman," said Norm's dad when Norm walked into the kitchen, scavenging for food.

Norm pulled a face. What was the big deal? He'd been out on his bike – not exploring a new flipping continent. "But..."

"What?" said Norm's dad.

"I live here," said Norm. "And it's lunchtime."

"Yes, but we were just talking about you, love," said Norm's mum.

Norm looked at his mum anxiously. They'd been talking about him? About the letter? About him not doing his homework? What did she have to go and tell his flipping dad for?

"About this iPad," said Norm's dad.

"What?" said Norm.

"Your mum says you need one."

Norm was temporarily lost for words. This wasn't quite what he'd been expecting.

Norm's mum smiled. "What did you think we'd been talking about, love?"

"Erm...dunno, Mum."

Norm glanced at his mum again. She winked. It looked like their secret was safe for the time being.

"Is that right, Norman?"

"What, Dad?"

"That you need an iPad? Or want one, anyway?"

"Er, yeah. 'Spose so."

"You **suppose** so?"

"No, I do, Dad," said Norm. "I definitely do, Dad."

Norm's dad scrutinized Norm for a few moments. "Why?"

Why do I want an iPad? thought Norm. Why does night follow day?

Why does six come between five and seven?

Why did the flipping chicken cross the road?

150

He just flipping wanted one and that was all there was to it! (An iPad. Not a chicken.)

"Your mum said something about apps," said Norm's dad.

"What?" said Norm.

"For your homework?" said Norm's dad.

"Oh right, yeah," said Norm, wishing his dad would hurry up and cut to the chase. Was he going to get one or not?

"We'll put fifty per cent towards it," said Norm's dad, as if he could read Norm's mind.

"We?" said Norm's mum, looking at Norm's dad pointedly.

"Your mum will," said Norm's dad.

"Really, Mum?"

Norm's mum nodded. "There's a chance the job could be made permanent."

"Right," said Norm, looking **and** sounding less than thrilled.

Norm's mum sighed. "I work in a cake shop, love. I'm not a footballer."

"Yeah, I know."

"I can't buy you one just like that."

Yeah, thought Norm. He knew why as well. If his mum bought him an iPad she'd have no money left to buy flipping weight-reducing spoons or whatever from the shopping channels she spent so much time watching. Maybe if she got off the flipping sofa from time to time she wouldn't actually **need** to lose weight.

"I'll pay for the whole thing initially. But you'll have to pay me back half."

Norm knew that he was expected to say something. But he also knew that if he said what he was really thinking, his mum might change her mind.

"Does that sound fair?" said Norm's mum.

No, it flipping doesn't, thought Norm. But then nothing ever **did**.

"Well?" said Norm's dad.

"What?" said Norm.

"You could be a bit more grateful!"

"But..."

"But **what**, Norman?"

Wasn't it obvious? thought Norm. Obviously not!

"Where am I going to get the other fifty per cent from?"

"That's your problem," said Norm's dad.

"Thanks," muttered Norm. "For nothing."

"Take it or leave it," said Norm's dad. "It's entirely up to you."

Norm really didn't have any choice. And frankly,

even if he did, his decision would have been exactly the same.

"I'll take it."

"Good," said Norm's mum.

"Thanks, Mum."

"You're welcome, love," said Norm's mum.

"And for...you know."

Norm's mum winked again.

"What's going on?" said Norm's dad.

"Nothing," said Norm's mum.

"Norman?"

"What, Dad?"

"What's going on?"

Norm shrugged. "Nothing, Dad. Honest."

"Hmm," said Norm's dad, seemingly unconvinced.

The front door slammed. The next moment, Brian suddenly burst into the kitchen like a bad smell, closely followed by John like an even worse one.

"Get that thing out of here!" shrieked Norm's mum.

"Yeah, get out, Brian," said Norm.

"I'm talking about the dog!" said Norm's mum.

"Aw, Mum?" said Brian.

"You heard your mother," said Norm's dad. "Out!"

John's grasp of English was still fairly basic, but he knew enough to know when he wasn't wanted, and slunk out of the kitchen with his tail between his legs.

"He peed next to the fridge the other day!" said Norm's mum.

"Who did?" said Norm. "John or Brian?"

"John," said Norm's mum.

"Maybe he can't help it," said Norm.

"What do you mean?" said Norm's dad.

"Dunno," said Norm, smiling at Brian. "Maybe he's subconsciously upset."

If Norm's mum or dad knew what Norm was referring to, they didn't let on.

"Well, Norman?"

"Well what, Dad?" said Norm.

"That money's not going to earn itself."

If only, thought Norm.

"I just saw an advert in the newsagent's window," said Brian.

"What for?" said Norm's mum.

Brian shrugged. "Dunno. Just did."

Norm's mum smiled. "I meant, what's the advert actually *for*?"

"Oh, right," said Brian. "For a paperboy."

Norm was confused. "There's a paperboy for sale?"

"Not for *sale*, you doughnut!" laughed Brian. "They *need* a paperboy! Or girl."

"I knew that's what you meant," said Norm.

Brian raised his eyebrows.

"What?" said Norm. "I flipping did! And by the way, who are **you** calling a doughnut, Brian, you flipping freak?"

"Language," said Dave, appearing in the doorway.

Norm spun round. "And you can shut up, Dave!"

"What's that you've got there, love?" said Norm's mum, spotting something in Dave's hand.

"Some leaflet that just got delivered," said Dave. "It's got a picture of Mikey's dad on it!"

"Let me see," said Norm.

Dave handed Norm the leaflet. Sure enough, there was a photo of Mikey's dad, grinning away like a lemon.

"What does it say?" said Brian.

"It doesn't say anything," muttered Norm. "You

have to read it."

"You know what he means, love," said Norm's mum. "Read it. Out loud."

"'PCs Gone Mad!'" read Norm. "'Your byte-size, local IT guy! Software upgrades and repairs. No job too small.'"

"Hmm, interesting," said Norm's dad. "Perhaps he could take a look at the computer, Norman?"

"What?" said Norm, beginning to panic.

"Perhaps you wouldn't actually *need* an iPad then."

"No, Dad!" yelled Norm. "You don't understand!"

Norm's dad grinned. "In that case I'd go and see about that job as quickly as poss—"

Norm didn't bother hanging around for lunch – or even to hear the rest of the sentence. He was out the front door and halfway down the drive before his dad had even finished saying it.

CHAPTER 15

The newsagent's was only a few minutes away by bike if Norm chose to take the most direct route from his house. Whenever he went on errands for his mum or dad though, he'd usually take anything **but** the most direct route – generally involving a detour via the woods at the back of the precinct. Unless of course there was something in it for him. And on this occasion there most definitely was. On this occasion there was potentially an iPad in it for Norm. Incentive indeed to get there as quickly as possible!

Norm pedalled furiously down the road, visions of bike-related apps and watching endless biking videos on YouTube crowding his head. All that guff about apps for doing his homework was precisely that. Guff. There was more chance of Norm marrying Chelsea than there was of him ever using his iPad to do his homework on. And there was no chance of *that* ever happening. He just couldn't flipping wait. No longer would he have to share the prehistoric family PC with his little brothers. No longer would he have to wait for up to thirty  seconds in order for something to download. Thirty seconds? Half a flipping minute? Frankly, it was outrageous, thought Norm. How had he tolerated it for so long? Never mind kids being shoved up chimneys in flipping Viking times or whatever. That was **nothing** compared to what Norm had had to put up with for as long as he could remember. Abso-flipping-lutely nothing!

Reaching the newsagent's in record time, Norm skidded to a halt and leaped off his bike. As he opened the door and walked inside, an electronic beeper beeped, prompting the newsagent to look up from the magazine she was reading.

"Yes, young man? And what can I do for you?"

More than you'll ever know, thought Norm.

"Well?"

"I've come about the job," said Norm.

"Have you now? And what job would that be?"

What did she mean, what job? thought Norm. What job did she think? The one as a flipping astronaut?

"The paperboy job?" continued the newsagent.

"Or girl," said Norm, recalling his conversation with Brian.

The newsagent smiled. "Make your mind up."

"Boy," said Norm.

"Sure?"

"Sure," said Norm.

"Hmm, paperboy, eh?" said the newsagent, eyeing Norm up and down.

Norm felt as if he was a bit of fruit in a supermarket. Any minute now he half expected her to squeeze him to see if he was ripe.

"Have you done a paper round before?"

Norm hesitated. Should he tell a porky and pretend that he had, in order to get the job? Or should he tell the truth?

"I'll take that as a no, then," said the newsagent. "I presume you know round here?"

Norm pulled a face. "Round where?"

"This area?"

"Oh, right," said Norm. "Er, yeah."

"Really?"

"Really," said Norm, deciding that it was probably best not to mention that it wasn't all that long since he'd moved from a completely different part of town and that he still occasionally got lost on the way to the toilet.

"Hmm," said the newsagent again.

So far, it had to be said, things weren't going quite as planned. Norm had assumed that all he had to do was show up and say he wanted the job and it would be as good as his. It never occurred to him that he was going to get grilled like a flipping kipper.

"You start Monday."

"What?" said Norm. "I mean, pardon?"

"You start Monday," said the newsagent.

"So I've got the job then?" said Norm.

"If you want it?"

If he wanted it? thought Norm. Flipping right he wanted it! He wanted it like nothing he'd ever wanted before. Or at least since the last time he'd really wanted something.

"Seven o'clock sharp," said the newsagent.

Norm was confused. Had he misheard? "Pardon?"

"Seven o'clock sharp."

Norm hadn't misheard. "At night?"

"In the morning."

This had to be some kind of joke, thought Norm. If so, it just wasn't funny.

"Seven o'clock in the morning? The actual morning?"

The newsagent smiled. "What time can you make?"

Norm thought for a moment. "Quarter to eight?"

"And would you like whipped cream and marshmallows on your hot chocolate?"

"Yes please, that would be lov—"

Norm suddenly stopped. She was being sarcastic. And he'd fallen for it like a complete doughnut.

"Here," said the newsagent, handing Norm a sheet of paper. "It's a map of the route."

"Thanks," said Norm.

"You **do** know how to read a map, don't you?"

"Yeah, of course," said Norm.

"You've got it upside down."

Norm laughed nervously and turned the map the right way round. "I knew that."

"Have you got a bike?"

Norm nodded. Had he got a bike? Did prawns pee in the sea?

"I'll give you a week."

A week? thought Norm. How long **was** this flipping paper round? He'd better take sandwiches.

"You're on trial."

"Oh, I see," said Norm. "Right."

"We'll see how it goes after that."

"'Kay," said Norm.

"See you on Monday morning then."

"See you on Monday morning," said Norm.

"Seven o'clock sharp?"

"Seven o'clock sharp," said Norm, heading for the door. "And thanks."

CHAPTER 16

"Morning, love," said Norm's mum, breezing into Norm's bedroom and pulling open the curtains to reveal a bright blue sky without a cloud in sight.

"Morning, Mum," mumbled Norm without bothering to look up from the mountain-biking magazine he'd had his nose stuck in ever since he'd woken up.

"Which do you want first? The good news or the bad news?"

Makes a change, thought Norm. Normally it was a case of which did he want first – the rubbish news or the even **more** rubbish news?

"Erm, the good news please, Mum," said Norm, finally looking up.

"I've ordered your iPad."

"What?" said Norm, scarcely able to believe what he was hearing. "Really?"

Norm's mum nodded and broke into a big, beaming smile.

"**Yesssss!**" said Norm, punching the air with one fist. This wasn't merely **good** news! This was fantastic news! This was amazing news! This was in-flipping-credible news! He was **finally** getting an iPad! Yee-flipping-ha! "Where from, Mum?"

"What's that, love?" said Norm's mum absent-mindedly, picking up a lone sock from the floor.

"Where did you order it from?"

"One of the shopping channels."

Course she did, thought Norm. Silly question really. But it didn't matter. His mum could have ordered it from a Chinese takeaway for all Norm cared.

"It's the latest one."

"When will it be here?"

"Hopefully by the time you get back from school tomorrow."

What? thought Norm. **Tomorrow**? Anything could happen before tomorrow! OK, so it probably wouldn't. But that wasn't the point. Tomorrow was in the future. Tomorrow was, like, science flipping fiction or something. Frankly, his mum might as well have said the year three flipping thousand!

"Why not **today**, Mum?"

"Because today's **Sunday**, that's why, love."

Norm sighed with resignation. It was **so** unfair. This had to be one of the best moments of his life so far. But there still had to be a flipping downside, didn't there? There always flipping was. It was flipping typical.

"Want to know what the **bad** news is?"

"Uh?" said Norm. "You mean **that's** not the bad news?"

Norm's mum laughed. "No, love. That's not the bad news."

Norm sighed with, if anything, even **more** resignation than before. "Go on then."

"You still have to do your homework."

"What?" said Norm, as if he'd just been told to cut the grass with a cheese grater.

"You heard."

Norm's mum was right. Norm **had** heard.

"Aw, you're joking, Mum!"

"I'm not, love."

"But..."

"But what?"

"I'm supposed to be checking out my paper round route. Make sure I know where to go and stuff."

Norm felt quite pleased with himself for coming up with a perfectly feasible excuse on the spot. He hadn't thought of sussing out the route before now. But actually, come to think of it, it wasn't such a bad idea. Anything to get out of doing his homework!

"So what are you doing in bed still?"

"What does it look like?" muttered Norm.

"Pardon?" said Norm's mum.

"Er, I said it looks like I'd better get up then, Mum," said Norm.

"Yes, you better had, love. It's past eleven."

"Really?" said Norm. "Whoa!"

"We don't want any more letters of concern now, do we?"

Norm's mum gave Norm one of her looks. Norm knew immediately what she was getting at. Furthermore, Norm's mum *knew* that Norm knew immediately what she was getting at.

"Have you still not told Dad?" said Norm.

Norm's mum shook her head. "Not yet, no."

"Not *yet*?" said Norm. "You mean…"

Norm's mum raised her eyebrows. "Better get cracking on that homework, hadn't you?"

17

Norm had no idea whether it was a rhetorical question or not. But one thing was for sure. Resistance was futile. He was going to have to do his homework sooner or later. Preferably later.

"Well?" said Norm's mum.

"'Kay, Mum," said Norm, putting down the biking magazine and flinging back the duvet.

CHAPTER 17

Norm was sat at the computer when he heard the tell-tale creak of the creaky floorboard. It had to be one of his brothers. If his mum or dad wanted something they usually just yelled from the bottom of the stairs.

CREAK!

"What?" snapped Norm irritably.

"How long are you going to be?" said Brian.

"As long as I flipping want," muttered Norm.

"But..."

"But what?"

"I need the computer."

"Well, tough, Brian," said Norm. "So do I."

"But..."

"Clear off, Brian!"

"But..."

"Are you still here?"

"Course I'm still here," said Brian. "Where did you think I was?"

Norm took a deep breath. There was a part of him that knew he should really be very grateful to Brian. If it hadn't been for Brian telling him about the paperboy job, Norm would never have known about it, let alone actually got it. It was, however, a pretty small part. The rest of Norm found Brian as deeply annoying as ever.

"Brian?" said Norm quietly.

"Yeah?"

"Clear off."

"What do you say?" said Brian.

"Please?" said Norm.

"No," said Brian.

"What do you mean, no?"

"Don't want to."

Norm took another deep breath. "I'm trying to do my homework here."

"Doesn't look like you're doing your homework to me," said Brian. "Looks like you're looking at bikes."

It was true. Norm *was* looking at bikes. Or more accurately, *drooling* at bikes. Bikes that he knew

he wouldn't be able to afford if he was still doing a paper round when he was ninety. And anyway, thought Norm, how was he supposed to do his homework when he'd just heard he was getting an iPad the next day? It wasn't just **hard** to concentrate. It was im-flipping-possible to concentrate!

"I could be doing a project," said Norm, not terribly convincingly.

"Are you?" said Brian.

"That's not the point!" said Norm, irritation levels rapidly beginning to rise again.

"Is that your homework?" said Brian, spotting a jotter and an exercise book on the table next to the computer.

"Yes," said Norm.

"Maths, eh?"

"Yes, maths," said Norm.

Brian looked at the jotter more closely.

"That's not right," said Brian.

"What isn't?" snapped Norm.

"Question three," said Brian. "'Calculate the value of angle y'."

"What about it?"

"Well, the angles in a triangle always have to add up to a hundred and eighty degrees."

Norm pulled a face. "What if it's a really *big* triangle?"

"Doesn't make any difference," said Brian. "They still only add up to a hundred and eighty. The angles in this one add up to about five hundred."

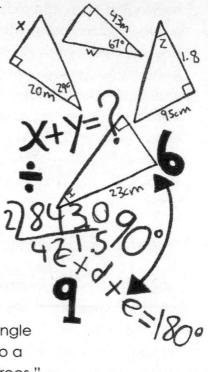

Norm sighed. He couldn't make up his mind what he was more miffed about – the fact that Brian was still showing no signs of leaving him in peace, or the fact that even though he was nearly three years younger than Norm, Brian was about ten times better than him at flipping maths!

"Number four's wrong too."

"Uh?" said·Norm.

"It's the square of the ***hypotenuse***."

"What?"

"It's ***hypotenuse***," said Brian. "Not hippopotamus."

"Yeah, whatever, Brian!" said Norm.

Brian looked hurt. "I'm just trying to help."

"Yeah, well, don't!"

"Sorry," said Brian.

"Bed-wetter," muttered Norm under his breath.

"What did you just say?" said Brian.

"You heard," said Norm.

There was the very
briefest of pauses
before Brian's
face suddenly
crumpled like a
burst balloon and he
bolted towards his room
in floods of tears.

Just for a moment, Norm felt ever so slightly guilty.
But the moment soon passed. Norm's only regret
now was not saying it sooner. If he had, he might
have got rid of Brian a lot earlier!

CHAPTER 18

It was well after lunch before Norm was finally able to suss out his paper round. Or at least that's what he set out to do. But there wasn't a cloud in the sky. What was Norm supposed to do? **Not** go biking or something? Frankly, even if there **had** been a cloud in the sky, it wouldn't have made the slightest difference.

It could have been foggy.

It could have been blowing a gale.

There could have been six feet of snow.

Norm would have still got bored and gone biking instead.

So it wasn't exactly a **major** surprise when Norm bumped into Mikey in the school playground again. To be fair, he **had** actually sussed out the first part of the route. Well, the first street anyway. OK – the first couple of houses. But it was a start. And anyway, it wasn't Norm's fault that he had the attention span of a chair.

"All right, Norm?" said Mikey, jamming on his

brakes and executing a perfect hundred and eighty degree skid.

"All right?" said Norm, doing a wheelie and trying desperately not to look **too** impressed. It never ceased to be annoying though. The fact that it was **Norm** who was really into bikes and biking – but **Mikey** who was actually just that little bit better at it.

"What you up to?"

Norm shrugged. "Same as you by the looks of things."

"I'm supposed to be delivering leaflets, but I got a bit distracted," grinned Mikey.

"Yeah, me too," said Norm.

Mikey looked puzzled. "You're delivering leaflets?"

"Nah. Got a paper round."

"Cool!" said Mikey.

"That's brilliant, Norm. Nice one!"

"Thanks," said Norm.

"Erm, so..."

"What?"

"Where are the papers?" said Mikey.

"Uh?" said Norm. "Oh right. No, I'm just learning the route."

"Right," said Mikey.

"Well I was, anyway," said Norm. "Before I got... you know...thingied."

"Distracted?" said Mikey.

"Yeah, that's it," said Norm distractedly. "Distracted."

"So are you going to get..."

"An iPad, yeah," said Norm, saving Mikey the bother of actually having to finish the sentence himself.

"Excellent!" said Mikey. "When?"

"Tomorrow," said Norm.

"Tomorrow?" said Mikey. "Whoa! Must be *some* paper round!"

Norm pulled a face. "What do you mean?"

"If you can afford to buy an iPad after just one day!"

"Uh?" said Norm. "No, you doughnut! I've made a deal with my parents."

Mikey grinned. "I was just joking, Norm."

"I knew that," said Norm.

"I know you knew that," said Mikey.

They looked at each for a moment. They both knew that Norm didn't know that.

"What kind of deal?" said Mikey, getting the conversation back on track.

"They stump up half. I stump up the other half."

Mikey nodded approvingly. "And it's being delivered tomorrow?"

"Yup. Fingers crossed," said Norm.

"Nice one, Norm," said Mikey. "Nice one."

"'Bout flipping time," said Norm.

Mikey laughed. "Talking about delivery."

"What about it?" said Norm.

"I'd better get on and deliver these leaflets, I suppose," said Mikey, setting back off in the direction he'd just come from.

"Oh yeah. Right," said Norm, suddenly remembering what **he** was supposed to be doing and setting off after his friend.

Norm had a sudden thought. "Mikey?"

"Yeah?"

"Have you ever thought of..."

"What?"

"You know?"

"No. What?" said Mikey.

"Just dumping them?"

"What? The leaflets?"

"Yeah," said Norm.

"Are you serious, Norm?"

"Be much easier."

"Yes, but…"

"No one would ever know," said Norm.

"**I'd** know, Norm!"

"Yeah," said Norm. "But apart from you…"

"It would be completely immoral!" said Mikey.

"Yeah? So?" said Norm.

"I wouldn't be able to look my dad in the eye!"

It wasn't easy, cycling **and** shrugging at the same time. But Norm somehow managed it. "Why would you want to look your dad in the eye?"

"I'm going to pretend we never had this conversation, Norm," said Mikey frostily.

Norm couldn't for the life of him see why Mikey was getting so uppity.

And anyway, Mikey could pretend all he liked that they hadn't had the conversation. They still flipping had.

By now they'd reached the school gates.

"Good luck with the paper round," said Mikey, heading down the road.

Oops, thought Norm, who'd forgotten – *again* – what he was supposed to be doing. But before he could say anything, his phone rang.

"Hi, Mum," said Norm, fishing his phone out of his pocket and answering. "Tea time? What? Already? 'Kay, Mum. See you in a minute, Mum. Bye, Mum."

Norm pocketed his phone again. It was beginning to look like he wasn't going to be able to suss out the route of his paper round beforehand after all. He'd just have to turn up at the newsagent's the next morning and hope for the best. But that was OK, thought Norm. How hard could it actually be?

CHAPTER 19

Norm knew that he was awake. He just couldn't be bothered to open his eyes. It was way too early. He was far too tired. It really was too much of an effort.

The reason Norm knew that he was awake was because he'd stopped dreaming that he was being chased through the woods by a pack of zombie badgers from Mars – or whatever the correct term for more than one zombie badger from Mars was. At least, Norm **assumed** it was a dream. If it wasn't then he was in **big** trouble.

Norm gradually became aware that it was light outside. Even through his closed eyelids he could make out shifting shapes and random patterns. Slowly but surely, he also became aware that something was supposed to be happening that day. Something good. Something **very** good. And then it suddenly hit him. Like he'd walked into a wall.

He was only getting a flipping iPad!

Norm opened his eyes and stared at the ceiling. He could still hardly believe it. But it was true all right. He really **wasn't** dreaming. Of course, he was going to have to wait until after school to actually get his hands on it. But even that was OK. It would make the moment, when it finally arrived, all the sweeter. Nothing could possibly spoil today, thought Norm. Not his brothers. Not his mum and dad. Not even Chelsea. Today was going to be awesome. Abso-flipping-lutely awesome. Like Christmas come early. But way better.

The house was full of the usual early-morning sounds. A toilet flushing here,

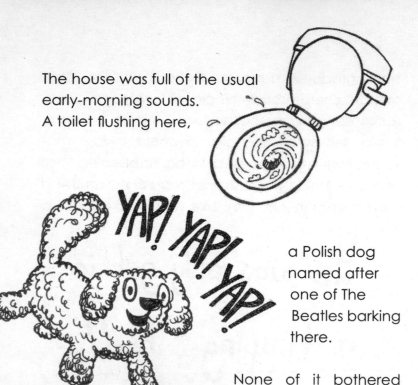

YAP! YAP! YAP!

a Polish dog named after one of The Beatles barking there.

None of it bothered Norm though. Not even the incessant chirping of the DJ oozing out of the radio in the kitchen and floating up the stairs like cheesy fog bothered Norm. Not today it didn't.

Norm rolled over and looked at the alarm clock on his bedside table. There was no time. Literally no time. For some reason the red digital numbers weren't where they normally were. The display was blank. Funny, thought Norm. Where had the time gone? And why was he getting a weird feeling in his stomach all of a sudden? Was it hearing the toilet flushing? Something was niggling Norm. But what?

Alarm bells began to ring. At least in Norm's head they did, anyway. The alarm clock on the table appeared to have died. Norm picked it up and gave it a shake. But it made no difference.

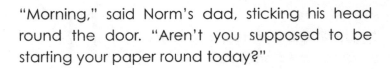

There was a knock on Norm's bedroom door.

"Come in," said Norm.

"Morning," said Norm's dad, sticking his head round the door. "Aren't you supposed to be starting your paper round today?"

Oops, thought Norm, gawping at his dad like a gobsmacked goldfish. At least that explained what the weird feeling in his stomach was.

"Norman?"

"Yeah, Dad?"

"Why are you looking at me like that?"

"Like what, Dad?"

"Like that."

"Erm..."

"Please don't tell me you've forgotten," said Norm's dad, the vein on the side of his head beginning to throb.

OK, thought Norm.

"What time are you supposed to be at the newsagent's?"

"Seven o'clock," said Norm.

"Seven o'clock?"

Norm nodded.

"In that case, I suggest you get a shift on," said Norm's dad, looking at his watch.

"Why? What time is it, Dad?" said Norm.

"Quarter past."

Norm pulled a face. "There's loads of time."

"Not quarter past six," said Norm's dad. "Quarter past seven."

Flip, thought Norm, doing his best to remain calm. At least on the outside. On the inside his vital organs were going completely ballistic. But he didn't want to give his parents any reason to suspect that he might not be able to keep his side of the bargain. Not when there was an iPad depending on it!

"And Norman?"

"Yeah?" said Norm.

"You're allowed to start panicking anytime you want."

"Thanks, Dad," said Norm, leaping out of bed and getting dressed without even bothering to take his pyjamas off first.

"What happened to your alarm clock, by the way?" said Norm's dad.

"That's what I'd like to flipping know!" said Norm, rushing headlong out the door and straight down the stairs.

CHAPTER 20

It didn't take long for Norm to wish that he hadn't allowed himself to get distracted the previous day when he was supposed be familiarising himself with his paper round. After three houses, to be precise. Still, that was three more houses than it looked like he was going to be delivering papers to at one point. For some reason, the newsagent didn't seem to think that a malfunctioning alarm clock was a good enough excuse to be late. Norm was just being honest though. He could have easily made up some excuse and pretended that he'd been abducted by aliens on the way or something.

But he didn't. And she actually had the nerve to threaten him with the sack if it ever happened again? How was Norm supposed to know if his flipping alarm clock was ever going to mal-flipping-function again? What was he? Flipping psychic or something? There was just no pleasing some people.

Norm yawned and looked around. Not only was he still half asleep, but he had no idea where he was. It didn't help that in his rush to get dressed and get out the door he'd forgotten to take the map with him. Not that the map would have helped much anyway, of course. Norm was about as good at reading maps as he was at reading Greek. He had enough difficulty telling his right from his left – never mind his north from his flipping south.

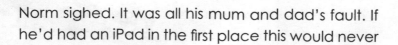

Norm sighed. It was all his mum and dad's fault. If he'd had an iPad in the first place this would never have happened. He could have opened up an app and instantly known *exactly* where he was. Then again, thought Norm, if he'd had an iPad in the first place, he wouldn't be *lost* in the first place, because he wouldn't be doing a flipping paper round in the first place! It was *SO* unfair. And *SO* flipping annoying!

"What are you looking at?" said Norm, spotting a cat sitting on the bonnet of a parked car, staring at him.

"First sign of madness, that, *Norman*! Talking to yourself."

Gordon flipping Bennet, thought Norm. That was *all* he flipping needed!

"I'm not talking to myself. I'm talking to the cat."

"Oh, well, that's completely different then," said Chelsea. "Nothing mad at all about talking to a cat. Sorry. Didn't mean to interrupt, *Norman*."

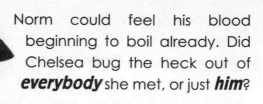

Norm could feel his blood beginning to boil already. Did Chelsea bug the heck out of ***everybody*** she met, or just ***him***?

"Don't let me keep you," muttered Norm.

Chelsea looked at the cat for a moment and then back at Norm.

"Oh, sorry. Didn't realise you were talking to me."

"Very funny," said Norm. "What are you doing here, anyway?"

"I live here," said Chelsea.

"What?" said Norm.

"I live here," said Chelsea. "On this street. With my mum."

"Oh, right," said Norm.

"I'm only technically your neighbour at weekends."

"Lucky me," muttered Norm.

"What was that, **Norman**?"

"Nothing," said Norm.

"Anyway what are **you** doing here?"

"What does it flipping look like?" muttered Norm. "I'm delivering papers. Or **trying** to."

"Really?" said Chelsea.

"What do you think this bag's for?"

"I just thought you were making some kind of fashion statement," said Chelsea. "Quite suits you, actually."

Norm immediately blushed.

"Why have you gone red, **Norman**?"

It was a good question, thought Norm. Why **had** he gone red? He didn't **want** to go red! It was **so** flipping annoying!

"Gotta go."

"Aw, must you?" grinned Chelsea.

Norm couldn't think what else to say. It didn't matter though, because at that moment his phone rang. Norm could hardly get it out of his pocket and answer quick enough.

"Hi, Mikey."

 cooed Chelsea.

Norm glared at Chelsea. Could he not even talk to his mate on the phone without her chipping in? Apparently not.

"What?" said Norm irritably. "Yes, I **know** I'm late, Mikey! Flipping alarm clock didn't work, did it?"

"Language," said Chelsea.

"Shut up," said Norm.

"Ooooooh!" said Chelsea sarcastically.

"Not you, Mikey," said Norm. "I was talking to Chelsea."

Norm closed his eyes for a few seconds, then opened them again. But it was no good. She was still there.

"You're funny," giggled Chelsea.

"What?" said Norm.

"When you get angry," said Chelsea. "It's very funny."

Norm took a deep breath. So Chelsea found it funny when he got angry, did she? In that case she was going to have a **really** good laugh any second now because Norm was on the verge of losing it, big time.

"What?" said Norm.

"I said it's..."

"Not you," snapped Norm, cutting Chelsea off. "What did you just say, Mikey?"

Norm's face suddenly dropped. And he was in a bad enough mood already.

"French homework?
OF course I flipping haven't!!
I didn't even know we'd
got any French homework!!"

"*Quelle dommage*," said Chelsea.

"Shut up!" hissed Norm.

"Ooh la la!" said Chelsea sarcastically.

"No, Mikey! Not you!" said Norm. "What time is it, anyway?"

"*Il est huit heures vingt-cinq*," said Chelsea.

"Uh?" said Norm.

"Twenty-five past eight."

Gordon flipping Bennet, thought Norm. Twenty-five past eight? This wasn't going well. This wasn't going well at all. He was late. He had no idea where he was. He still had a bagful of newspapers to deliver. And now he'd just found out he'd got flipping French homework? He hadn't even had breakfast yet! This was already shaping up to be a seriously rubbish day. Even by Norm's standards! And that was flipping saying something!

Norm thought for a moment. He was going to have to dump the papers somewhere. He didn't care if it was immortal or whatever Mikey reckoned it was. What else was he supposed to do? And anyway, he could always go back and get them after school. He could still deliver them. They'd just be a bit late, that was all. It was no biggie.

"I've got an idea," said Chelsea.

Norm glared at his occasional next-door neighbour. He had an idea too. How about she kept her flipping nose out of where it wasn't flipping wanted?

"I'll do it," said Chelsea.

"What?" said Norm.

"I'll do it."

"You mean..."

"Deliver the rest of the papers, yeah," said Chelsea.

"But..."

"But what, **Norman**? You couldn't possibly let me do it for nothing? Well that's very generous of you."

"Erm..."

"If you absolutely *insist*," said Chelsea. "How does fifty–fifty sound?"

"What?" said Norm, who felt as if he was rapidly being bulldozed into a corner.

"Fifty–fifty," said Chelsea. "Half your wages. That's fair, isn't it?"

"You mean half of *today's* wages?" said Norm.

Chelsea laughed. "What? No, no, *Norman*! Half of your *week's* wages!"

Norm could hardly believe what he was hearing. She wanted *half* of his entire week's wages for helping him out for *one* day? Not even a *whole* day? *Part* of a day? It really was abso-flipping-lutely scandalous. On the other hand, Norm had to admit, it was also pretty flipping impressive. And probably precisely what he would have done too, if things had been the other way round and he'd been Chelsea. Which, thank goodness, they weren't. And which, thank goodness, he wasn't.

"So what do you say, **Norman**?"

Norm looked at Chelsea. What **did** he say? Because no matter how badly she was attempting to rip him off, she was also basically offering to dig him out of a massive hole. OK, so he'd only end up with half the money for this week's paper round. But it was either that, or probably not even **having** a paper round this time next week. He really didn't have much of a choice.

"Can I just check something?"

"Go for it," said Chelsea.

"This is a straight business transaction, right?"

"Totally," said Chelsea.

"I don't have to feel, you know...grateful or anything?"

"Nah," said Chelsea.

Thank goodness for that, thought Norm. It was bad enough Chelsea actually helping him. The thought of then having to feel indebted to her afterwards was too much to bear.

"Well?" said Chelsea. "Do we have a deal, *Norman*?"

Norm nodded. "Deal."

"Excellent," said Chelsea. "In that case you'd better give me that bag, hadn't you?"

Norm handed Chelsea the paper bag, trying not to look *too* relieved. But actually it *was* a relief. In more ways than one.

"It's heavier than it looks, isn't it?" said Chelsea.

Norm tried to look nonchalant. "Can't say I noticed."

Chelsea smiled. "Ooh, you're so strong, *Norman*!"

Norm could feel himself blushing again.

"Is that somebody shouting?" said Chelsea.

"I can't hear anything," said Norm.

"Listen," said Chelsea.

They listened.

"Norm!" said a faint voice.

"It sounds like Mikey to me," said Chelsea.

"What? Oh right, yeah."

Norm had completely forgotten that he'd been talking to Mikey. Or at least *trying* to anyway.

yelled Mikey at the top of his voice, at the exact moment when Norm put the phone back to his ear.

"FLIPPING HECK!!!" screamed Norm. "No need to shout, Mikey! You just about blew my flipping head off!"

Chelsea burst out laughing.

"Shut up!" snapped Norm. "Not you, Mikey!"

Chelsea laughed again.

"You going, or what?" said Norm.

"All right, **Norman**!" said Chelsea, heading off. "Keep your hair on!"

"What's that, Mikey?" said Norm, watching her go. "Yes I **know** I'd better get a shift on! But thanks for reminding me."

Gordon flipping Bennet, thought Norm, ending the call and pocketing his phone again.

The cat sitting on the car bonnet meowed pitifully.

"And you can shut up, too!" said Norm.

CHAPTER 21

Norm just knew he was going to be late for school that morning. It wasn't exactly rocket science. Sure enough, Norm **was** late. For registration **and** for his first period. Which just happened to be French.

"***Ah, bonjour, Norman!***" said Mr Lewis – or Looroll as he was known to pupils – when Norm eventually appeared in the doorway.

"What?" said Norm, making his way to his desk and sitting down.

"***Bonjour***," said Mr Lewis. "***Ça va?***"

Norm pulled a face. French, it had to be said, wasn't his strongest subject. It wasn't even in the top ten. "Erm…"

"*Quelle heure est-il?*" said Mr Lewis.

"*Oui?*" said Norm without much conviction.

"*Non*," said Mr Lewis. "*Quelle heure est-il?*"

Norm thought for a moment. What was that thing Chelsea had said earlier?

"*Quelle fromage?*"

Someone laughed. Norm knew without even looking that it was the new kid, Clint Westwood – who seemed to be keen, not only to impress and suck up to every single teacher, but also to annoy Norm with his whiny, know-it-all voice.

"Clint?" said Mr Lewis.

"*Oui, Monsieur?*" said Clint.

"Would you care to translate for Norman, please?"

"Certainly," said Clint.

Norm gritted his teeth. Frankly, he couldn't care **less** if Clint translated for him or not. As far as Norm was concerned, there was more point in geography and history than there was in flipping French. And there was no point whatsoever in geography and history.

"You said to Norman, '*Quelle heure est-il?*' which means 'What time is it?'" said Clint. "And **Norman** replied '*Quelle fromage?*' which means 'What cheese?'"

This time, pretty much the whole class laughed – including Mr Lewis. Even Norm could see the funny side. Not that he was going to admit **that** to anyone.

Especially Clint flipping Westwood!

"What you **meant** to say was '**Quelle dommage**', meaning 'What a pity,'" said Mr Lewis.

"Not that **that** would have made any sense either," Clint chuckled.

Whatever, thought Norm. And anyway, how did Looroll know what he'd meant to say? He **might** have meant to say cheese! No one could prove that he hadn't!

"So, Norman?" said Mr Lewis.

"Yes?" said Norm.

"Yes, what?" said Mr Lewis.

"Yes, Mr Looroll," said Norm. "I mean, Mr Lewis."

There was a deathly silence. No one dared laugh.

"Homework?"

Oops, thought Norm. Not only had he forgotten

to do his French homework in the first place, he'd actually **forgotten** that he'd forgotten to do his French homework in the first place. And Mikey had only just told him!

"What about it?" said Norm.

"Have you **done** it?"

"Erm, not exactly," said Norm.

"Not exactly?" said Mr Lewis. "What's that supposed to mean?"

"It means he hasn't done it," sniggered Clint.

"Shut up!" said Norm.

"Well?" said Mr Lewis. "**Have** you?"

"Done it, you mean?" said Norm, knowing perfectly well what Mr Lewis meant, but desperately stalling for time.

"Yes," said Mr Lewis.

"No," said Norm.

"No?" said Mr Lewis.

"Not yet," said Norm.

"Not **yet**?" said Mr Lewis. "But it was for today."

"Yeah, I know," said Norm.

Mr Lewis sighed. "This isn't the first time, is it, Norman?"

Norm shook his head.

"What's your excuse?"

Norm thought for a moment. It had worked once, hadn't it? Why wouldn't it work again?

"Computer's rubbish."

"**Sorry?**" said Mr Lewis.

Norm nodded. "Yeah, so am I."

"That's not what I meant," said Mr Lewis. "Are you saying that it's not **your** fault you haven't done your homework, it's your computer's fault?"

"Yeah," said Norm. "Keeps crashing. It's rubbish."

Mr Lewis sighed again. "You don't **always** have to use a computer to do your homework, you know."

"Yeah, I know that," said Norm. "You can use an iPad as well."

Mr Lewis took a deep breath. "That's not quite what I meant either, Norman."

But Norm wasn't listening any more. All Norm could think about was getting home as quickly as possible after school, and hoping there'd be a parcel with his name on it when he got there. Or a parcel with his mum's name on it, anyway. Nothing else mattered to Norm at that moment. He didn't even notice Mr Lewis writing on a sheet of paper, before folding it and popping it in an envelope.

"*Voila*," said Mr Lewis.

"Uh?" said Norm.

"*Pour vos parents*," said Mr Lewis, handing Norm the letter.

Quelle flipping *dommage*, thought Norm.

CHAPTER 22

There was no chance of Norm dawdling back
from school today, or killing time by going via the
allotments. Norm couldn't get home fast enough.
Frankly, if he'd thought he could have got away
with riding his bike straight into the house instead
of into the garage, he would have done.

"Well?" panted Norm, bursting into the front room without bothering to take his helmet off.

"I'm fine thanks, love. How are you?" said Norm's mum without bothering to take her eyes off the TV.

"All right," said Norm.

"How was school?"

"All right," said Norm.

"Anything to tell me?"

"Er, don't think so, Mum, no," said Norm, desperately hoping that the next question wouldn't be about any letters he might or might not have received.

"Any homework?"

"Bit of French."

"Bit of French, eh?"

Norm nodded. Not that his mum could actually *see* him nod. She still hadn't taken her eyes off the TV.

"And will you be needing the computer to do this so-called bit of French?"

"Yeah, about that, Mum," said Norm.

"About what, love?"

"Has anything...?" said Norm, leaving the rest of the sentence hanging in the air.

"Has anything what?" said Norm's mum.

"Arrived?" said Norm.

"What do you mean?" said Norm's mum.

Norm wanted to scream. What did his mum flipping *think* he meant? Would this torture never end? Could she not *see* what she was doing to him? Well, of course she couldn't. She *still* hadn't taken her eyes off the flipping TV!

"A package?"

"A package?" said Norm's mum, like this was the furthest thing from her mind.

Norm nodded pointlessly again.

"Funny you should say that, love."

"Is it?" croaked Norm, like a toad with tonsillitis.

"Here," said Norm's mum, handing Norm a package.

"Yesssssss!" said Norm.

"What do you say?"

"'Bout flipping time!" said Norm, frantically tearing at the cardboard.

"Pardon?" said Norm's mum.

"What the heck?" yelled Norm.

Norm's mum finally turned round to find Norm holding a spoon.

"Oh. Sorry, love."

Sorry? thought Norm. Was that *really* all his mum had got to say? For building his hopes up like that and then smashing them to smithereens? This had to be some kind of sick-minded wind-up. Either that or he was dreaming. Norm closed his eyes. But when he opened them again he was still holding a flipping spoon.

"Is this what you were looking for, Norman?" said Norm's dad from the doorway.

Norm spun round to see his dad, holding another package and grinning like a doughnut. He turned back to his mum. She was grinning like a doughnut too.

"Brilliant," said Norm's dad. "I told you he'd fall for it, didn't I?"

Norm's mum nodded.

"Ha, ha, very funny," said Norm.

"I wish I'd got a camera," said Norm's dad.

"I wish I'd got different parents," muttered Norm under his breath.

"What was that, Norman?"

"Nothing, Dad."

"Here you go," said Norm's dad, handing Norm the package.

"Thanks, Dad."

Norm's mum and dad watched expectantly as Norm turiously began to tear open the package.

"Well?" said Norm's mum.

"What do you think?" said Norm's dad.

Norm didn't quite know **what** to think. "Is this another joke?"

Norm's mum pulled a face. "No, why? What do you mean, love?"

Norm hesitated. Almost as if he couldn't quite believe what he was about to say.

"It's..."

"What?" said Norm's dad. "Amazing? Fantastic? Incredible? The best thing ever?"

"**Pink**," said Norm.

"What?" said Norm's dad.

"It's pink," said Norm.

"Pink?"

Norm took a deep breath and exhaled noisily. What part of **pink** did his dad not flipping understand?

"Look," said Norm, finally producing the iPad from the debris of the packaging.

"He's right," said Norm's dad. "It **is** pink."

"Oops," said Norm's mum.

Oops? thought Norm. This was a bit more than flipping oops! This was oops with fries! This was a complete and utter disaster on a previously unimaginable scale. This was...

"I didn't **mean** to!" said Norm's mum.

I should flipping hope **not**, thought Norm. It was bad enough **accidentally** ordering a pink iPad – let alone ordering a pink iPad on purpose!

"What's wrong with pink anyway?"

"You serious, Mum?" said Norm. "For an iPad?"

Norm's mum shrugged. "Why not?"

Norm thought for a moment. His mum was right. Why not have a pink iPad? In fact why stop there? Why not make being caught in possession of pizza a criminal offence?

Why not make it compulsory to walk backwards with your pants on your head? Why not make fish wear flipping goggles? There were some things that just **weren't** right. And a pink iPad was one of them!

"If you're that bothered, get a cover for it," said Norm's mum. "No one will ever know!"

"*I'll* flipping know!" said Norm.

"Language," said Dave, suddenly appearing out of nowhere.

"Shut up, Dave," said Norm.

"Is that a pink iPad?"

Norm sighed. "**Yes**, it's a pink iPad."

230

"Cool," said Dave.

"No, Dave. Not cool," said Norm. "Not cool at all."

"When am I going to get my Stynx?" said Dave.

"When I get some money," said Norm.

"When will that be?"

"When I get paid."

"When will that be?" said Dave.

"Dave?" said Norm.

"Yeah?" said Dave.

"Don't talk to your brother like that, Norman!" said Norm's dad. "Apologise to him!"

"What?" said Norm.

"You heard," said Norm's dad. "Apologise. Now!"

Norm couldn't quite believe it. As far as he was concerned, *he* was the victim here. He was the one who'd been wronged. He was the one who'd been pooped on from a great height. Not Dave. And yet, for some reason, it was Norm who was having to apologise! It was *SO* unfair. And *SO* flipping typical!

"Sorry, Dave," mumbled Norm.

"That's all right," grinned Dave. "That's four cans you owe me now."

CHAPTER 23

Norm needed to get away from the house after tea. If he didn't, he knew there was a very good chance that he'd explode from sheer frustration. Also, he didn't particularly want to be asked any tricky questions about why he suddenly owed Dave four cans of Stynx.

Mikey's place was the obvious destination. It usually was when Norm just wanted to chill. Mikey's house was a strictly stress-tree zone. An oasis of sanity. A

haven of calm. Well, compared to Norm's own house it was, anyway. The closest thing to a full-blown crisis at Mikey's was the time Mikey's mum couldn't make hot

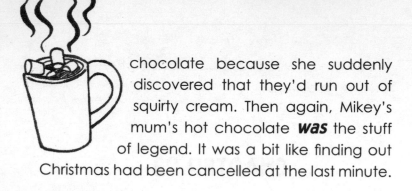

chocolate because she suddenly discovered that they'd run out of squirty cream. Then again, Mikey's mum's hot chocolate **was** the stuff of legend. It was a bit like finding out Christmas had been cancelled at the last minute.

"Oh, hi," said Mikey, answering the door.

"Hi," said Norm.

Norm and Mikey looked at each other for a moment.

"Do you want to come in?"

"No, Mikey. I want to stand out here like a complete doughnut, you doughnut," said Norm. "Course I want to come in."

Mikey stood to one side as Norm brushed past him and headed straight up the stairs.

"Wasn't expecting to see you tonight, Norm," said Mikey, walking into his bedroom to find Norm already sat down and on the Xbox.

"Yeah, well, I wasn't expecting to be here myself, was I?" said Norm.

"Why? What's happened?"

"Don't ask."

"Really?"

"Really **what**?" said Norm.

"You really don't want me to ask?" said Mikey. "Or are you just saying that?"

Norm sighed. If he'd wanted his head nipped he could have stayed at home. But he might as well spit it out and tell Mikey now that he was here. If he didn't, the chances were that Mikey would start banging on about how they were best friends and how they were always there for one another and all that guff, and frankly Norm just wasn't in the mood.

"You really want to know, Mikey?"

Mikey nodded. "I really want to know, Norm."

"It's about the iPad," said Norm.

"Hmm, thought it might be," said Mikey. "Did it not arrive or something?"

"Oh, it arrived all right."

Mikey pulled a face. "So what's the problem?"

Norm turned to face Mikey. "I'll tell you what the problem is. It's pink. That's what the problem is."

"Pink?"

"Pink," said Norm.

"A pink iPad?"

Norm nodded. "A pink iPad."

"I didn't even know you could **get** a pink iPad!" said Mikey.

"Neither did I," said Norm gloomily.

"Maybe it's a limited edition," said Mikey.

Norm snorted. "Not flipping limited enough!"

"Seriously, Norm. You ought to hang onto it," said Mikey. "It could be worth a fortune in years to come!"

Norm looked at Mikey. "Are you off your rocker?"

"I was just…"

"I don't care **how** much it might be worth in years to come, Mikey!

It's a flipping pink iPad!"

"Bummer," said Mikey.

"Is the **correct** answer!" said Norm as if he was a quiz show host on TV.

"So is she sending it back, then?"

"What?" said Norm.

"Is your mum sending the iPad back?"

"No, Mikey, she's keeping it," said Norm.

"What?" said Mikey.

"Course she's flipping
sending it back, you
doughnut!"

"All right, all right," said
Mikey. "I was only asking!"

Norm sighed. "Sorry."

"It's OK, Norm."

"I'm just a bit..."

"Honestly, it's fine," said Mikey. "I'd be upset if I
were you."

"You mean upset about the iPad?" said Norm. "Or
just generally upset if you were me?"

Mikey laughed.

"It's **SO** flipping unfair."

"I can imagine," said Mikey.

Yes, thought Norm. And that was all Mikey would **ever** have to flipping do as well. Imagine. Nothing unfair ever happened to Mikey. Mikey didn't have tight-fisted parents. Mikey didn't have annoying little brothers. Mikey didn't have a part-time next-door neighbour seemingly hellbent on making his life as miserable as possible. What had Mikey got to complain about? Nothing as far as Norm could see. Abso-flipping-lutely nothing!

"There's nothing wrong with pink though, Norm."

"What?" said Norm.

"Nothing," said Mikey.

"No, come on, Mikey. What did you say?"

Mikey suddenly looked uncertain. As if he wasn't sure whether to say what he was about to say or not.

"Pink's not just for girls," mumbled Mikey, staring at his feet. "That's..."

"What?" said Norm.

"Thingyist."

"***Thingyist?***" said Norm.

"Don't make me say it, Norm."

"Say what?"

Mikey glanced at the door to make sure no one was there.

"Sexist."

Norm was horrified. It was easy to forget that Mikey was just that little bit older and had already turned thirteen. And if something was easy to forget, Norm usually forgot it.

"That is so **gross**, Mikey!"

"Well, it *is*," said Mikey.

Norm had a thought. Talking of being older and hormones and stuff. "You haven't got any spare cans of Stynx I could borrow, have you?"

Mikey smiled. "Borrow? Or have?"

Norm *almost* smiled. "Have."

Mikey hesitated. "Maybe."

"Mikey?"

"Yeah?"

"Have you, or not? I really need to know."

Mikey nodded. "Yeah."

"Excellent," said Norm. "Can I have some then?"

"How many?" said Mikey, opening his wardrobe.

"Four."

"No problem."

"Thanks," said Norm. "You're a pal."

"You'll pay me back, won't you?" said Mikey, producing four cans of deodorant from a drawer and giving them to Norm.

"Course I will."

"When?"

Norm suddenly remembered the deal he'd struck with Chelsea that morning.

"Could be a while yet, Mikey."

CHAPTER 24

Getting up on time the next morning wasn't a problem for Norm. Norm's dad made sure of that by banging loudly and repeatedly on his bedroom door.

"Gordon flipping Bennet!" yelled Norm, falling out of bed, convinced that if the world hadn't actually just ended, it was about to.

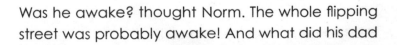

"Are you awake in there?"

Was he awake? thought Norm. The whole flipping street was probably awake! And what did his dad mean, was he awake *in **there***? Where else would he be awake? Belgium?

"Come on, up you get," said Norm's dad, sticking his head round the door but soon wishing he hadn't bothered. "Phwoar! What have you been doing in here, Norman? It smells disgusting!"

"One who smelt it dealt it," muttered Norm, getting to his feet.

"It wasn't me!" said Norm's dad.

"He who denieth supplieth," muttered Norm.

"Better not light a match!" said Norm's dad. "The whole house would go up like a rocket!"

Really? thought Norm. Interesting.

"Don't even **think** about it, Norman. And for goodness' sake open a window. I'm surprised you can actually breathe in here!"

Norm pulled back the curtains and peered outside. If he hadn't felt like doing his paper round before, he **definitely** didn't feel like doing it now. It was pouring with rain.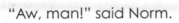

"Aw, man!" said Norm.

"What is it?" said Norm's dad.

"Do I **have** to, Dad?"

"Do you have to what?"

"Do my paper round."

"What?" said Norm's dad. "Well, of course you do!"

"But..."

"No buts, Norman!"

"But…"

Norm's dad sighed. "What?"

"It's peeing it down!"

"Pardon?"

"It's **peeing** it down!" said Norm, a bit louder.

"Do you mean it's **raining**, Norman?"

"Whatever," said Norm. "I'm not going out in that!"

"You're not serious, are you?"

Norm pulled a face. Was he serious? Course he was serious! It was horrible out there! What was he? A flipping penguin or something?

"Norman?" said Norm's dad, the vein on the side of his head beginning to throb.

"Yeah?"

"You've **got** to do your paper round!"

Norm shrugged. "Have I?"

"What do you mean, have you?" said Norm's dad, his voice getting higher and higher. "What's the alternative?"

What was the alternative? thought Norm. The alternative was **not** doing it. The alternative was going back to bed and getting another hour's kip in before he had to go to school. The alternative was...

"Dad?"

"What?"

"Can you drive me round?"

"Pardon?" said Norm's dad.

"Can you drive me round?" said Norm.

"You mean in the car?" said Norm's dad.

No, thought Norm. In the flipping dishwasher!
Of **course** he meant the flipping car!

"Please, Dad?"

Norm's dad stared at Norm. Slowly but surely, he
began to smile. "That's funny, Norman. That's very
funny."

"But..."

"Please don't say it."

Norm looked puzzled. "Don't say what, Dad?"

"That you're not joking."

"But I'm not," said Norm.

Norm's dad took a deep breath and exhaled slowly. "Give me one good reason why I should drive you."

This was looking promising, thought Norm. Or if not actually **promising**, it wasn't a straight no either. His dad must be **thinking** about it, at least. That was good. It was a start anyway.

"One reason?" said Norm.

Norm's dad nodded. "One reason. Oh, and Norman?"

"Yeah?"

"Me being a sucker doesn't count as a reason. OK?"

"'Kay, Dad," said Norm.

"Well?" said Norm's dad. "I'm waiting."

Norm was waiting too. But in Norm's case, he was waiting for inspiration to suddenly strike. This was his big chance. And he couldn't afford to blow it. Why should his dad drive him round his paper round? Why not? It wasn't like he'd got anything **better** to do! It wasn't like he had a job or anything. Not since...

Hang on a sec, thought Norm. That was it! **That** was the one good reason!

"Er, Dad?"

"Yes, Norman?"

"Remember when you, er..."

"What?"

"'Left' your old job?" said Norm, making speech marks in the air with his fingers.

Norm's dad immediately looked uneasy. He knew exactly what Norm was referring to. Being sacked. More importantly, never telling Norm's mum that he'd been sacked – pretending instead that he'd been made redundant. There was a difference. A big difference. Norm knew that. Norm's dad **knew** that Norm knew that. Norm **knew** that his dad knew that Norm knew that.

"What about it?" said Norm's dad.

"Dunno," said Norm nonchalantly. "Just thought maybe you still owed me a favour? For not telling Mum?"

Norm's dad fixed Norm with a look. "Are you blackmailing me, Norman?"

"Dunno," said Norm mysteriously. "You tell me."

Norm's dad was confused. "You don't know whether you're blackmailing me or not?"

"Erm..." said Norm, who was starting to get pretty confused himself.

"Let me get this straight," said Norm's dad. "If I drive you round, you won't tell Mum about me getting...well, you know..."

Norm nodded. "Yeah. I mean, no. I mean, that's right."

Norm's dad looked out the window. If anything the rain had started to fall even more heavily.

"I don't know, Norman. It doesn't seem right to me."

Norm looked pleadingly at his dad. It seemed very right to **him**! In a funny way, he'd actually be doing his dad a favour. He didn't get out much. It might even help him to feel better about himself. Improve his self-esteem and all that guff!

"OK, OK," said Norm's dad. "Just this once?"

"Just this once, Dad."

"Then we're quits?"

"Then we're quits, Dad."

"No more favours?"

"No more favours," said Norm.

Norm's dad shook his head and set off for the door. "Come on then. Let's get on with it."

"'Kay, Dad," said Norm, starting to get dressed.

"I don't know," said Norm's dad as he disappeared out the room. "I must be mad."

"Not mad," muttered Norm to himself. "Just a complete sucker."

CHAPTER 25

Norm's dad waited in the car whilst Norm ran into the shop.

"Well, well, well," said the newsagent, looking up from her magazine as the door opened and the electronic beeper beeped.

What, what, what? thought Norm.

Well, Well, Well

"I wasn't expecting to see **you** today."

Norm laughed nervously. "Really?"

"Not after yesterday's performance, no," said the newsagent.

Uh-oh, thought Norm. Perhaps letting Chelsea do his round hadn't been such a good idea after all.

"Would you like to explain what happened?"

Not really, thought Norm.

"Well?" said the newsagent.

"Erm..." said Norm.

"You can't just dump the papers behind a hedge!"

What? thought Norm. But...

"I've never **had** so many complaints!"

Norm sighed. He might have flipping known Chelsea would pull a fast one. Some people were just **SO** flipping unreliable!

"Well?" said the newsagent. "What have you got to say for yourself?"

It was a good point, thought Norm. What **had** he got to say for himself?

"Er, I needed the toilet."

"Pardon?"

"I needed the toilet. So I hid the papers and went home."

The newsagent listened, increasingly incredulous. Even Norm realised it didn't sound terribly likely. But he'd started now, so he might as well finish.

"When I went back I couldn't find them."

"You couldn't find them?"

"I couldn't remember where I'd hidden them," said Norm.

The newsagent sighed. "You **do** want the job, don't you?"

Norm nodded vigorously. Of course he wanted the job. Well – **needed** the job. For now, anyway. Once he'd earned enough money to pay for half an iPad she wouldn't be seeing him for flipping dust!

KERCHING!

"You'd better pull your socks up then, hadn't you?"

Norm nodded again as the door opened and the beeper beeped.

"Is there a problem?" said Norm's dad from the doorway.

Norm turned round. "It's OK, Dad."

"Is this your son?" said the newsagent.

No, thought Norm. He went round calling **everybody** Dad!

"Guilty," said Norm's dad.

Charming, thought Norm.

"I was just telling him how he needs to pull his socks up if he wants the job permanently."

"Oh, really?" said Norm's dad.

"Yes, well, he didn't exactly get off to the best start yesterday."

"And why's that, then?" said Norm's dad.

"He lost the papers."

Norm's dad pulled a face. "Lost them?"

"It wasn't my fault!" said Norm.

"Well, it certainly wasn't mine," said the newsagent.

"I think you're being a bit harsh," said Norm's dad, the vein on the side of his head beginning to throb.

Norm was taken aback slightly. He wasn't used to his dad defending him. He and his dad were usually on complete opposite sides when it came to arguments. Or most things for that matter. Could this be some kind of fresh start? Some new phase of their relationship? Probably not, thought Norm. But he might as well enjoy it while it lasted.

"Really?" said the newsagent. "You think I'm being harsh, do you?"

Norm's dad nodded. "I do actually. He's only twelve, for goodness' sake."

Everything suddenly went very quiet.

"Pardon?" said the newsagent.

"I said he's only twelve," said Norm's dad.

"Nearly thirteen," mumbled Norm.

"I had no idea," said the newsagent.

Norm shrugged. "You didn't ask."

"No, but I should've done."

"What?" said Norm.

"You have to be thirteen to do a paper round."

"But I'm *nearly* thirteen," said Norm.

"Doesn't matter."

"Right," said Norm. "So…"

"I'm going to have to let you go."

Norm pulled a face. What did she mean, she was going to have to let him go? It sounded like he was being released back into the flipping wild or something!

"Are you **sacking** me?" said Norm.

"I wouldn't quite call it that," said the newsagent.

Really? thought Norm. Because it **sounded** like he was being sacked to him. Sacked! Before he'd even got the job! Flipping typical!

"Might you be able to...bend the rules a little?" said Norm's dad.

The newsagent looked at Norm's dad like he'd just farted the national anthem.

"**Bend** the rules?"

"It wouldn't be for **long**," said Norm's dad. "They'd never find out!"

Who? thought Norm. The Ministry of flipping Paperboys?

"Sorry, but that's not possible," said the newsagent. "Now if you'll excuse me, I need to find somebody who **can** deliver these newspapers. *Legally*."

Norm's dad thought for a moment. "I'll do it."

"Really?" said the newsagent.

Norm's dad smiled. "Nah, not really. Come on, Norman."

Norm watched as his dad disappeared out of the shop, along with any last, lingering hopes he still had of being able to pay for half an iPad.

CHAPTER 26

"Thanks **very** much, Dad," said Norm, getting out of the car and trudging up the path.

It was the first time Norm had spoken since they'd left the newsagents and driven the short distance home. Or Norm's dad had driven the short distance home anyway. Norm had spent most of the journey sulking and staring out of the window with a face like a badger's backside.

"Are you being sarcastic, Norman?"

Norm sighed. "Yes, Dad, I'm being sarcastic."

"Why?"

"Why do you *think*, Dad?"

"I've no idea. That's why I'm asking."

Gordon flipping Bennet, thought Norm, watching as his dad opened the front door.

"What did you have to go and do that for?" said Norm, following his dad into the hallway.

Norm's dad looked puzzled. "What? Open the door?"

"No!" said Norm. "Tell her how old I am!"

"Oh, I see. So *that's* what you're in a mood about!"

Well, duh! thought Norm. What did his dad *think* he was in a flipping mood about? He was in a mood because he'd just been sacked! And it was all his flipping dad's fault! The newsagent was all set to give him another chance. But no. His dad just **had** to open his big trap, didn't he? He just couldn't help himself. And now Norm no longer had a job. Well, at least that was one thing he had in common with his dad!

"That was quick, love," said Norm's mum, appearing at the foot of the stairs.

"Didn't do it," muttered Norm darkly.

"What?" said Norm's mum.

"The paper round."

"Why not?"

"Ask **him**," said Norm with a tilt of his head.

Norm's mum turned her attention to Norm's dad.

"Well?"

"He's too young," said Norm's dad. "You need to be thirteen before you can do a paper round.

"Really?" said Norm's mum.

"No, not really, Mum," said Norm.

"Pack that in!" snapped Norm's dad.

"Pack what in?" said Norm.

"Being sarcastic!"

Norm's mum smiled
sympathetically.
"That's a shame,
love. You must be
very disappointed."

Very disappointed?
thought Norm.
That was *one* way of
putting it. He could think
of several other ways of
putting it too, but decided
that it was probably better not to say anything at
the moment.

"Have you sent it back yet, Mum?"

"The iPad?" said Norm's mum. "Not yet, no."

"Buy you're going to, right?" said Norm anxiously.

"Of course, love."

"No point looking for another one," said Norm's dad.

Norm was gobsmacked. "What do you mean, Dad?"

"Well, you're not going to be able to pay for half of one *now*, are you?" said Norm's dad. "Mum might as well get her money back. She doesn't exactly earn a fortune you know, Norman."

"Earns more than you flipping do," muttered Norm.

"What was that?"

"It's your fault, Dad," said Norm.

Norm's dad looked at Norm, the colour visibly draining from his face.

"What's your fault?" said Norm's mum, turning to his dad.

"Erm..." said Norm's dad.

Norm smiled at his dad's obvious discomfort. He clearly thought Norm was about to spill the beans about him getting sacked from his *own* job. Norm might not be getting an iPad any time soon – but he was determined to enjoy this moment for as long as he could.

"What's Dad's fault?" said Norm's mum, turning to Norm.

Norm hesitated. It was tempting. Very tempting. But in the end, he couldn't quite bring himself to do it.

"It's Dad's fault they found out how old I am, at the newsagent's."

"Oh, I see," said Norm's mum.

Norm's dad breathed a huge sigh of relief.

"What did you **think** I was going to say, Dad?"

"Nothing," said Norm's dad casually.

"Breakfast, anyone?" said Norm's mum, heading for the kitchen.

"Great," said Norm's dad, following.

"Thanks for the Stynx, Norman," said Dave, suddenly appearing at the foot of the stairs.

Norm pulled a face. How did Dave know about that? He hadn't seen him since he'd got back from Mikey's the night before.

"Have you been in my room again?" said Norm.

Dave grinned.

"You have, haven't you, you little freak?"

Dave shrugged. "Might've been. Why? What are you going to do about it?"

"I'll think of something," said Norm.

"I'm not sure that's a good idea," said Dave.

"Why not?" said Norm.

Dave suddenly produced an envelope from his back pocket.

"That's why not."

Norm looked. It was a letter. Not just any old letter. The letter from Mr Lewis, his French teacher. The one he'd managed to avoid talking about. The one his parents hadn't seen. So far, anyway.

"Gimme that," said Norm, trying to grab the letter.

"No chance," said Dave, dodging out of the way and heading for the kitchen. "That's another two cans of Stynx you owe me by the way, Norman!"

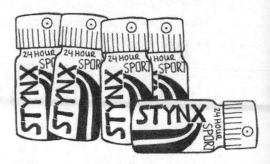

"What?" said Norm.

"Unless you want me to...?"

"OK, OK," said Norm. "Please, Dave, don't..."

But it was too late. Dave had gone. Norm sighed. Could the day actually *get* any worse? It wasn't even eight o'-flipping-clock yet!

"Have you done your paper round already, Norman?" said Brian, coming down the stairs.

"No," said Norm.

"Why not?"

"Because."

"What?" said Brian.

"Because I just flipping haven't, Brian, all right?"

"That's not a proper reason," said Brian.

"Shut up, you bed-wetter!"

Norm waited for Brian to run off in tears again. But he didn't.

How annoying, thought Norm. It looked like he was going to have to come up with a **different** way of insulting his middle brother from now on.

"You got up on time then, Norman?" said Brian.

"What?" said Norm.

"You didn't oversleep?"

"No," said Norm. "Why?"

"Ooh, no reason," said Brian. "Just wondering how your alarm clock was, that's all."

Uh? thought Norm. What did **Brian** want to know about his flipping alarm clock for? Unless...

Brian grinned.

Norm was up the stairs in a flash. A couple more strides and he'd reached his bedroom. A couple **more** strides and Norm was standing by his bedside table, frantically taking the back of the alarm clock off.

"The little..."

No flipping **wonder** the flipping alarm clock hadn't worked, thought Norm. Someone had taken the flipping batteries out! And Norm had a pretty good idea who that **someone** was.

CHAPTER 27

Norm couldn't be bothered with school that day. Not that Norm could *ever* actually be **bothered**. But that day, of all days, Norm *really* couldn't be bothered with school. From the moment he arrived and locked his bike up in the bike shed, he just couldn't wait to **unlock** it again and leave. So when the bell finally rang, Norm wasn't only the first out of the classroom, he was first out of the school gates as well.

There was no question in Norm's mind where he was going to go. He was going to go to the allotments and see Grandpa. Well, hopefully see Grandpa anyway. He wasn't quite sure why he wanted to go so much. It wasn't like Grandpa could wave a magic wand and suddenly make everything better. All Norm knew was that he couldn't face the prospect of going home. Not just yet anyway.

What was the point of going home? Apart from wreaking some kind of horrible revenge on Brian? And anyway, thinking about it, thought Norm, Brian only did it to pay him back. They were probably quits now.

OK, thought Norm, so discovering that Brian had **deliberately** sabotaged his alarm clock had been a surprise at the time. But it was really just the latest in a whole series of rubbish things that had happened lately. It was the straw that broke the camel's back.

Or the icing on the cake.

Or the icing on the cake that broke the camel's back...

or whatever that flipping expression was that Norm was trying to think of. It didn't matter. What mattered was the fact that Norm was no longer getting an iPad. Not unless some kind of miracle happened. And miracles tended **not** to happen. At least not in Norm's experience.

As Norm whizzed through the woods though, skidding round corners and zigzagging in and out of trees, he gradually began to feel better. Not massively better. But a bit better. Slowly but surely, Norm's cares and woes began to evaporate like steam from a kettle. He still had plenty of cares and woes left by the time he reached the allotments – but somehow Norm felt calmer. More chilled. Not quite as wound up as he had been earlier. Biking seemed to have that effect on Norm. It was like medicine. But medicine that Norm actually looked forward to taking.

Bike-o-ty!

Take 3 times

"Hi, Grandpa," said Norm, cycling up the allotment path. "I'm glad you're here."

"Oh, yeah?" said Grandpa,
looking up from the book he was
reading, sat on a chair outside
his shed. "Why's that then?"

Norm shrugged. "Dunno."

"You're glad I'm here but
you don't know why?"

"Not really, no," said Norm.

"Fair enough," said
Grandpa. "Glad we got
that cleared up."

Norm smiled. Grandpa could be a
bit like medicine too, sometimes.

"How's the job-hunting going?"

"Don't ask," said Norm.

"Too late," said Grandpa. "I just did."

Norm sighed. "You haven't heard then?"

"About what?"

"Me getting a paper round?"

"You've got a paper round?" said Grandpa.

"**Had** a paper round," said Norm.

"Oh, I see," said Grandpa. "That was quick. What happened?"

"The newsagent found out I'm too young."

"Really?" said Grandpa. "Bad luck."

"Tell me about it," muttered Norm.

"How?"

"How what?"

"How did the newsagent find out you're too young?"

Norm briefly wondered whether to tell Grandpa about Chelsea dumping the papers – but decided not to in the end. At the end of the day, it wasn't actually **Chelsea's** fault he'd lost his job.

"Dad told her," said Norm.

"Your **dad** told her?" said Grandpa, looking **and** sounding confused. "What did he do that for?"

"I've no idea!" said Norm.

"For goodness' sake," said Grandpa. "Never did like him."

"Who?" said Norm.

"Your dad," said Grandpa.

Norm laughed.

"It's true," said Grandpa. "Never understood why your mum wanted to marry him in the first place."

Norm couldn't understand why **anyone** would ever want to get married in the first place. Marriage, as far as Norm could see, consisted mainly of arguing about where you were going to spend Christmas

and traipsing round IKEA.
But that was another story.

"Still skint then?"

"Skint?" said Norm. "Never
been skinter!"

"That's a shame."

Norm nodded. "Yeah, it is a bit."

"Still want an iPad?"

"What?" said Norm.

"Still want an iPad?"

Did he still want an iPad? thought Norm. What
kind of ridiculous question was that? Grandpa
might as well have asked if he still wanted his
flipping elbows!

"Are you serious, Grandpa? Course I do!"

"Not much chance of that then, is there?"

Norm was beginning to wish he'd gone straight home after all.

"Unless..."

"Unless what, Grandpa?" said Norm.

"Hmmm," said Grandpa, stroking his chin thoughtfully.

"What?" said Norm.

"Nothing. I was just thinking, that's all."

"What?" said Norm.

"Nah, you probably wouldn't be interested, Norman."

Norm pulled a face. "I might be."

Grandpa hesitated. "I was just wondering..."

"Yeah?" said Norm.

"Well, the thing is..."

Gordon flipping Bennet, thought Norm. What was the thing?

"I'm not using mine."

"Your iPad?" said Norm, scarcely daring to believe what he was hearing.

Grandpa nodded. "Haven't even switched it on yet."

"But..."

"What?"

"What about all that family tree stuff?" said Norm.

"Pffff, what was I thinking?" said Grandpa. "Load of old nonsense. Who **cares** about ancestors? They're all dead anyway."

Norm looked at Grandpa expectantly. "So?"

"So I was wondering if you..."

 yelled Norm.

"I haven't finished yet," said Grandpa.

"Sorry, Grandpa," said Norm, barely able to breathe – let alone actually speak. So much for miracles not happening!

"Thank you," said Grandpa. "As I was saying…"

"Yeah?" said Norm.

"I was wondering if you and your brothers might like to…"

"What?" said Norm. "Did you say me and my—"

Norm stopped as soon as he saw the corners of Grandpa's eyes beginning to crinkle in the corners.

"Very funny, Grandpa. Very funny."

"There *is* a catch though, Norman."

Norm sighed. There just **had** to be a flipping catch, didn't there? It wouldn't be the same if there **wasn't**.

"What, Grandpa?"

"You're going to have to earn it."

 said Norm.

"See that spade over there?" said Grandpa with a tilt of his head.

Norm looked at where Grandpa was indicating. Sure enough, a spade was sticking out of the ground.

"You want me to fetch it for you?" said Norm.

"In your dreams, Norman."

"What?"

"I want you to get digging," said Grandpa.

"Seriously?" said Norm.

"Seriously," said Grandpa.

Norm sighed and headed for the spade. Some people were just **SO** unreasonable.

"Excuse me?" said Grandpa.

"What?" said Norm.

"Anything to say to me?"

Norm smiled. "Thanks, Grandpa."

"Hilarious stuff from one of my comic heroes!"
Harry Hill

Just when Norm thought life couldn't get any more unfair...

THE WORLD OF
NORM
MAY BE CONTAGIOUS

Coming soon!

ORCHARD BOOKS
www.orchardbooks.co.uk